Table of Contents

Table of Contents ....

Painted Ladies: a kaleidoscope of stories 2

COPYRIGHT & ACKNOWLEDGEMENTS 2

DEDICATION 2

CHAPTER ONE - INTRODUCTION TO THE COLLECTION OF STORIES 3

Kwickie Kaption 1 5

CHAPTER TWO - THE SITTING 6

CHAPTER THREE – JOJO'S EYES 9

KWICKIE KAPTION 2 29

CHAPTER FOUR – A HARD PLACE 30

CHAPTER FIVE – THE GHOST GOOSE 38

SECTION ONE – A Little Girl 39

SECTION TWO – Happy Families 48

SECTION THREE – Lottie in the World 58

SECTION FOUR – Aunt Lottie and Uncle Deet 67

SECTION FIVE – Lottie Sees The Goose 78

KWICKIE KAPTION 3 83

CHAPTER FIVE – THE ROUND TABLE 84

CHAPTER SIX – THE PAINTED LADY 92

KWICKIE KAPTION 4 140

CHAPTER SEVEN – ALADDIN'S CAVE 141

CHAPTER EIGHT – INSPECT & VERIFY 166

KWICKIE KAPTION 5 174

CHAPTER NINE – A TINY TURN 175

About Beth 183

Painted Ladies: a kaleidoscope of stories

COPYRIGHT & ACKNOWLEDGEMENTS

Many of the tales in this collection required months of research, both for accuracy and to create a credible ambience. Although I take full responsibility for any inadvertent errors, I am indebted to a dedicated group of eagle-eyed readers who helped on the journey.

The butterflies on the cover are known as Painted Ladies. I am indebted to Dr Jim Asher, Chair of Butterfly Conservation, dedicated to saving moth and butterfly species, for permission to use his beautiful photograph.

DEDICATION

When I first met him several decades ago, I had no idea that a friend could be so loyal, so ever- ready to offer an empathetic shoulder as well as an endless supply of shared laughter. It's with love and thanks that I dedicate this collection to my friend David James.

CHAPTER ONE - INTRODUCTION TO THE COLLECTION OF STORIES

Unless you already know why a collection of short fiction might feature butterflies on the cover, let me explain.

If you were as lucky a child as I was in the gifted toy department, you know the joy of holding a kaleidoscope to the light and creating infinite patterns of colour with each tiny turn. When I discovered that the generic term for a group of butterflies is also called a kaleidoscope, I thought it could make a good title. And tucked away in the store-room of my mind was an idea that could fit.

During the late 1950s of my teenage years I attended what the Americans call a public school, and the British know as a state school. The expectation was that most of us students would go on to higher education, and the curriculum during my four years of high school duly focused on academic preparation. I was in no position to judge at the time, but not only did the faculty take their task seriously, the most enlightened members introduced us to the joys of independent thought along with their specialized subjects. Intellectually I felt right at home with that approach; my own father constantly urged me to question everything and not just follow the crowd.

I recall a discussion about gender representation in the arts. We were asked to consider why there were so few women poets, painters and composers recorded throughout the centuries. Sadly, the conclusion appeared to be that the works of men were *a priori* superior. It's even sadder that as I write this in the run-up to 2020, such social misrepresentations persist.

In the world of painting alone, such pre-20th century artists as Gwen John, Berthe Morisot, Amelia Robertson, and Joan Carlile paved the way with consummate skill for later often astounding and innovative contributions. Spear-heading a huge and growing powerful list, Louise Bourgeois, Barbara Hepworth, Pauline Boty, Judy Chicago, Georgia O'Keeffe, Dame Rachel

Whiteread, and Tracy Emin easily put paid to any critical doubters.

I find it fascinating how musicians, writers, choreographers et al have been inspired by a single image to forge new creative paths. With *Painted Ladies,* images of and sometimes by women have become my own literary starting point, producing flash fiction, short and longer stories, and novellas, plus one tale bound around with historical accuracy. These are interspersed with comic memes, one-liners, a bit of a giggle.

The stories are illustrated by the paintings that inspired them, each with a paragraph or two about the artist. All have been re-titled and adopt a narrative voice loosely befitting time and place. A veritable literary kaleidoscope!

Kwickie Kaption 1

The ancient Egyptians believed that in order for a person's soul to survive in the afterlife it would need to have food and water. The opening of the mouth ritual was thus performed so that the person who died could eat and drink again in the afterlife.

OMG Cleo... this is the best costume party EV-VER!

Chapter Two - The Sitting

Painted by Angelika Kauffmann [1741-1807], one of the finest portrait and still life painters of the 18th century, this depiction of Dame Susannah Cullum bears testament to the respect allotted to her as one of the founders of Britain's Royal Academy.

The sitter's place in titled society, her family's acquaintance with royalty, and her past reputation as one of the beauties of her era, form the background to my story. In the form of a monologue, it reveals both actual references and presumptions of their effect on Lady Cullum, and I hope captures some of the unintentional humour of a woman both influential and not wholly intellectually rigorous.

Dame Susannah Cullum, Depicted in her 72nd year 1784

The Sitting

No, Frau Kauffmann, I do not want another cup of that dishwater you call coffee. Perhaps that is the beverage standard back in your native Switzerland, but I'd like to see you perch here for hours, enshrouded in frills and flounces, without moving a muscle and yet contrive to smile. How sprightly would you look? 'Tis no wonder I yawn and yawn again. Surely it is well gone the hour of the clock we agreed for this sitting.

I still cannot believe my son, Sir John, was so eager to recommend you for my portrait. So far as I know you started to paint him and then some inordinate time passed and your work remains unfinished. Leastways, no one's seen even a brushstroke of it. Too otherwise employed starting your Royal Academy I have no doubt.

You needn't scowl, Frau Kauffmann, 'tis most unbecoming. At seventy-two years of age and long past my majority, I assure you that time has not clouded the clarity of my mind, and one need not stick at one-and-twenty with wrinkles smothered in leaded powder to absorb the tittle-tattle of the day. Move my head where? To the left? No, I am sure it was at this angle. I'm not fussed what you claim to see... 'tis my neck after all!

As you of all people will be aware, I have been the subject of several portraits, and was considered a veritable rose, Frau Kauffmann, a very flower of womankind. So, yes, I say... A Royal Academy indeed! Quite an accomplishment, Madam, to gain the nod of the monarch, though in fairness they do whisper abroad he might be of madness taken, bless him, and who knows but the great and acclaimed Sir Joshua Reynolds may even have coaxed him to approve your venture. In truth, I have nothing against painters of the female persuasion, though best they stop within the walls of their own drawing room, and there contrive to depict a bowl of persimmons or favourite lap dog, before pecking out some tune on the clavier... but what on God's green earth inspired you to pose me with this heavy tome?

Is it meant to be the word of Our Lord, for the title cannot be read even by the most literate in the land? In any way or manner, how long exactly am I meant to hold it between two fingers? Who, I humbly ask you, just who holds a book like that? Could you? Were I given to wagering, I say you could not! Even Sir John, my son, the fifth Baronet, and as you are well aware, an ordained clergyman, even he... and I know him best that do know him at all... even he could not sustain a pose like that.

Do you believe, Frau Kauffmann, that merely because you are so intimately entangled with Sir Joshua... [oh, yes, I declare parenthetically, you needn't deny it, 'tis the scandal of our age, we know all about his secret name for you, Miss Angel. I thank the Good Lord my late husband was spared such goings on]... do you, I ask again, believe that you can dance around the civilities of society, laughing up your nose, and arranging us into impossible poses?

Far be it for me to impart any advice to a such a woman of the world as yourself, but it might be wise to ponder what the advancing years may bring. Yes, Frau Kauffmann, it comes to us all. I refer of course to old age, unless of course, some disease or accident precludes a natural ending. I do hope you, yourself, enjoy robust health.

Prithee, ring for your maid. I will take some fresh water, and then I must depart, Madam, before I come to the end of my breath and my words are squeezed past the end of this page.

***

CHAPTER THREE – JOJO'S EYES

Un Bar aux Folies-Bergère 1881/2 Édouard Manet

Manet's last major work, *Un Bar aux Folies-Bergère*, is universally held as a masterpiece of the late 19th century. For some historical context, its completion coincided with another outbreak of the Russian Flu, a virulent pandemic that had periodically raged over the world for some three hundred years.

With characteristic wit, Manet signed the label of the wine bottle set out for sale, alongside the English ale... the two nations had been allies in the recent ill-fated War of 1870, aka the Franco-Prussian War. The ambiguous setting not only evokes the venue itself, which kept its daily promise to entertain, but contrasts with those dreaming of escape.

At least two-thirds of the image is contained within a huge wall-mounted mirror reflecting the upper-loge of the auditorium. The whole ambience retains the grandeur of the hall's original construction as an opera house.

In the extreme left of the reflection are the lower legs of a member of an acclaimed acrobatic troupe, shod in trademark green boots, confidently balanced on his trapeze bar – begging the question that two bars feature in the painting.

From his perch the acrobat can not only view his audience, but he can focus on the woman behind the marble bar, her customers, and the refreshments arranged before her. With influential friends in literary circles, such as Proust and Zola, Manet was well aware of De Maupassant's contention that the dish of tempting oranges for sale tagged the woman as a "vendor of drink and of love."

Apparently the model for this barmaid was a prostitute called Suzon, who posed for the painting in Manet's studio. Some art analysts have noted the recurring triangular shapes throughout the image. The most startling example is the bright corsage atop the woman's neckline, which is almost perfectly replicated by the split at the bottom of the bodice, evoking a geometry of genitalia... the empty space to be filled in the viewer's imagination by the sensual bouquet.

Manet's work having been ignored for many years by the Paris Salon, the painting caused much controversy in its debut exhibition in 1882. It's even more remarkable an achievement because his leg had recently been amputated as a consequence of syphilis, and he suffered from agonizing phantom leg syndrome. My story picks specific details from the painting itself, but spins them into a completely fictional narrative. I've particularly been interested in contrasting levels of social deceit with the truth of genuine emotion. Taking cues from old time music hall and variety shows, I hope the presentation suggests both the boldness and charm of each successive act.

JoJo's EYES

VOICE OF THE BARKER

Mesdames et messieurs, vous êtes tous les bienvenus!! Bien, bien, bien. Venu, venu, venu! Don't be shy, right this way. Just two little francs gets you in, no questions asked, no reservation required. We're open twenty-four hours a day, every day, matinees and late into the night. Why stand out in the cold? Inside is every attraction you could wish for.

Relax before the show in The Grand Hall. Frites, patisseries, les oranges. If you can't afford the champagne deluxe, the coffee's strong, the beer even stronger, though the flesh is weak. Greet your friends and make some new ones, if you catch my drift. Regardez... There's a jolie fille all on her ownio. Don't be shy, Monsieur.

If you crave variety, we cater for every taste. Feeling classical? On vous propose Le Ballet Excelsior featuring the terpsichorean sensation Odette Valery. Recitations from the Bard of Avon et aussi, ecoutez moi, laugh until you cry at the wit of Le Nez, oui, c'est lui-même, Molière.

Are you an animal lover... and who ain't... Galletti's cheeky performing monkeys will tempt your smile. Quake and be terrified by Nala and her twisting, slithering snakes. More, you say? Who could resist Lockard's très amusant elephant orchestra dressed as clowns. And for you equine admirers, don't miss the horse-riding demonstration to rival Napoleon's Cavalry. Hold it right there, mesdames et messieurs. Stay right where you are for Monsieur Gordon's trained dogs - they jump through hoops, turn circles in the air, mon dieu, they're practically flying! Every night at eight.

The variety is endless. Et musique partout. Have you seen the butterfly dance of La Loie Fuller, who's charmed the crowned heads of the continent. Your toes will tap to the tunes of wasp-waist Polaire. Become ensnared by the wrigglings of Eugenie Fougère's seductive cakewalk; some swear claims of epilepsy, but it's the dance craze sweeping the nation. Jerk and wiggle, wiggle and jerk! Thrill to the trills of London's Lottie Collins and her Ta-ra-ra-Boom-de-ay. Marvel at the risqué ditties of the Barrison sisters and place your bets on where they've put their pussies. Are you blushing, madame?

Hurry, hurry or you'll miss the moment. We're all adults here. Surely nothing you've not seen before. You won't be shocked by the tableau vivant, so tastefully lit under spot-lamps of mauve and pink. Shapely women not moving a muscle, wearing only a smile, albeit very well upholstered front and behind, if you catch my drift. Better leave Grand-mere at home to look after les enfants.

Something for everyone. The treat supreme is Monsieur Joseph and his troupe of green-booted acrobats. Surely you've heard of the amazing JoJo! Up there, look... up near the ceiling. Daring, death-defying. He's got his eye on you. And you. And especially on you!

Don't be shy, mesdames, messieurs. Step right up. Admission's just two small francs. You won't find a better show than right here in Montmartre at the fabulous Folies-Bergère!

*

THE SADNESS OF SISTERS

Minette lays a cool cloth over her sister's forehead. "Please let me get a doctor, Claudie," she pleads. "Or at least a sage-femme."

Claudine's eyes are closed but her chest rises and falls with a steady rhythm. She waves away the prospect of doctors or midwives. Holding out her arms she says, “Give me the baby, my tits are killing me.”

Minette hesitates. If the baby suckles she’s bound to catch the flu with the milk. “Please, Min!” Her voice no more than a croak. She tries to sit up, and Minette props some pillows behind her head. Positioned at her mother’s breast, the little girl drinks eagerly.

“Monsieur Sarin?” She tries to cough away the rattle of her breath, but the pain in her ribcage cripples any movement, and she doesn’t want to distress the baby. “Has he said anything?”

“Haven’t seen him for weeks. Busy with his accounts, I’m betting.”

“Are we in trouble?” Minette knows that by ‘we’ she means the theatre itself, The House, as they call it. Claudine struggles back against the pillows. “She’s done,” she gestures to the baby, and Minette lifts her back to the cot. Her tummy full, the little one is already fast asleep. When she turns back to her sister, she can tell the moment between life and death has passed.

*

THE HEART OF JOJO

Even growing up they are mistaken for twins; they look so much alike it takes someone very familiar to tell them apart: Claudine, and Minette just a couple of years younger. JoJo has the vision. Was he born with it? Who can tell? Trained by the finest twisters and human tower-builders in the fabled Far East, a dedicated pupil of Mam’selle Aimée the Human Fly who walks on the ceiling, JoJo’s become an acrobat of supreme skill, discipline and some divine grace.

He flexes his knees and the tightrope trembles. Perched way up there, his legs almost welded to the trapeze, and with a view taking in the spectators all the way down to the blushing bar-maid serving in the upper loge alcove, he can see it’s Minette. But what has she stowed under the marble-topped bar?

Girls without dowries are always de trop for the poor, and so, when she’s trusted to travel and to ease the burden at home,

Minette joins her sister in Paris. Even the theatre manager Monsieur Sarin hasn't noticed, but it's nearly a month since she's filled in for Claudine. Somewhat reluctantly she helps out, tending the loge bar if Claudie falls ill or is offered a well-paid assignation lasting several days or longer.

She quickly realises how her sister makes her living. Don't be fooled by that air of rural innocence. The girls, playmates from birth, grow ever closer with the years. They never judge each other's choices, driven to escape the drudgery, the boredom of village life. To be sure, Claudine's path is more spiced with danger and shame, but Minette has bigger dreams. She fancies learning to design some of the stunning and outré costumes worn onstage, and has even approached one of the seamstresses to take her on as an apprentice.

It's a matter of love at first sight for JoJo, nursing his passion with silent patience over time. He leads the Troupe at the Folies and trots them far around the world… to the White Nights of the north, the big tops of Boston, and the bright lights of Blackpool. Unwavering devotion, and still she's unaware; considers him a good friend, un vrai copain.

Without any intention on her part, Minette masks his reason, blinding him to all others. He's obsessed, l'amour fou. He waves at her, planning the best way to meet up and find out what's going on with the sisters. Not wanting to scare her away, he imagines she's quite a fragile birdie, not toughened up to squawk in the face of danger like Claudine. As soon as he finishes setting up his equipment for the show, he can scoot under the stage, climb the internal stairs that lead directly to the refreshment alcove. Nobody the wiser.

*

CHECKING THE CAST LIST

It takes many hundreds of minions, assistants and entourages to satisfy the needs of star-studded divas and vedettes, not to mention meeting the expectation of the crowds. Monsieur Sarin has gathered a veritable village to keep the wheels oiled in The House. He trusts their expertise.

But have no doubts, among them all, JoJo and the sisters are the headliners in this story. No need to quieten the crowds in the gallery, or shush the toffs relaxed in their boxes. The orchestra is tuning up, resolving discordant notes into a harmonious tonic, signaling the show can well and truly begin.

Ladies with lorgnettes, gents peering through binoculars. Necks craned the better to view the stage, every eye blinking with anticipation. There, look! Voila! The heavy red velvet curtain rises on the glorious, notorious, wanting ever more-of-us... The Folies-Bergère!

Even if this is their first visit, everyone knows the format. The moment one act takes its final bow, gasps and applause unbound, then the spotlights dim, only to shine anew on the next. It's up to you whether to follow the variety on stage or chase it through the lively alleys of Montmartre.

Aside from a couple of walk-ons, only two other characters play their part. A man and a tiny newborn, neither with a name for our cast list; neither stamped onto the promotional posters. Oh, you'll know 'em when you see 'em. The Gentleman. Like all his kind, whether embarked from England's shores or sidling through the side streets of Pigalle, he's always turned out in the costume of his class.

Little if anything distinguishes him from the scores of men who accompany their partners or roam solo through the Great Hall seeking out refreshments and perhaps some company for the duration of the show. But look a bit closer, and you'll see that appearances are deceptive. He hasn't shown up at the Folies for nearly a year, so what, you may wonder, brings him here tonight?

You've already met the remaining person. Though tiny and yet to acquire a name, she catches us by her pungent odour. It not only advertises her full diaper, but pinpoints a particular and potentially lethal reminder. Like a mob of hooligans bent on destruction, Russian Influenza rages through the city, leaving the very air full of Sulphur and Satan. The whoops of the Folies crowd might drown out *sotto voce* whispers, but nothing can mask such a stench.

*

THE DOUBLE-ACT SKIPS ON

My dog has no nose, quips the comedian.
How does he smell? asks the feed.
Terrible!
Boom-Boom!
AND OFF THEY SKIP AGAIN

*

AN UNEXPECTED ADDITION TO THE ENTERTAINMENT

Ah, the Gentleman can drink, of course, but can he sing? Now here's a funny thing. JoJo knows, and Minette is learning. Sometimes there's an unscheduled lull in the night's running order. Could be a late arrival, a back-stage mix-up, whatever. Fear not, mesdames et messieurs, the Folies-Bergère is prepared. Whoever gets to the stage first becomes the next act. Beloved by the crowd, they cheer and whoop and stamp their feet. This time the spotlight illuminates one of their own.

Monsieur Sarin uses the wheeze to get himself out of a hole. His bacon's safe, and he doesn't have to reprint the programs or shell out one single sou on wages for these self-appointed troubadours. Tonight the Gentleman is well placed in an aisle seat just moments from the stage, but who knows why he rushes up to perform, to sing his heart out so far from home.

Up to full beam comes the circle of light, white and bright against the red velvet. The orchestra vamps till ready. And here he is, The Gentleman, with a tune wrapped around a tragic tale. I promised you a Ballad, mesdames et messieurs, and a Ballad you shall have.

So many to choose from. JoJo knows 'em all. Shanties that smell of the salt of the sea. Some ring with flint, marking the rhythm of picks and shovels that empty the earth below of its guts. Men with sooty cheeks, hauling buckets up top to fuel the flames in hearths all across the land.

In his travels on Burmese steamers booked out of Glasgow by Paddy Henderson's Flotilla Company, to the golden citadels of high Peru, and the tavernas of Catalonia, JoJo once opted for those heroic hymns. But ever since Minette stole his heart, he prefers ditties of sweet affection – "The girl I love is serving in the gallery, The girl I love is smiling up at me…"

To be honest, most balladeers sing of hearts snapped in two, of pure love dashed on the grounds of betrayal. Here's one from a few centuries ago. I think you'll find it instructive. It's the one The Gentleman is singing right now, just for you.

Up above, in the loge alcove, Minette is listening. And above her head, JoJo listens, too. Though neither can identify the Gentleman. Not yet.

*

A Song, on the Confeſſion and Dying

Words of *William Stevenſon*, Merchant, late of *North-Allerton*, in the County of *York*, aged 27 Years, who was executed at *Durham* on *Saturday* the 26th of *Auguſt*, 1727, for the barbarous Murder of *Mary Fawden*, near *Hartlepool* in the Biſhoprick of *Durham*; taken from his own Mouth the Night before his Execution, by a Perſon that went to viſit him while in Goal.

To the Tune of, *Since Cælia's my Foe.*

GOOD Lord! I'm undone, thy Face I would ſhun,
I've anger'd my God, and diſpleaſed his Son:
I dare not come nigh thy great Majeſty,
Oh! where ſhall I hide my poor Soul when I die.

Thy Vengence I dread on my guilty Head,
All Hopes of thy Mercy from me now are fled;
My poor ſinful Soul is filthy and foul,
And Terror and Horror in my Conſcience roll.

The Shame of my Race, and Mankind's diſgrace,
My Actions all over were wicked and baſe;
No Devil in Hell that from Glory fell,
Can now with my Blood-guilty Soul parallel.

Her Affections I drew, how could I embrue
My Hands in her Blood! Oh! my God, I do rue
The curſt helliſh Deed, I made her to bleed,
That never did wrong me in thought, word, or deed.

I us'd my whole art, 'till I ſtole her Heart,
And ſwore to befriend her, and ſtill take her Part,
Thus being beguil'd, ſhe ſoon prov'd with Child,
Which made her weep ſorely, but I only ſmil'd.

With ſighs and with groans with tears and with moans
She utter'd ſuch Plaints a would ſoften flint Stone;
Oh! where ſhall I hide my Shame oft ſhe cry'd,
Dear Sir, take ſome pity, and for me provide.

I fear'd ſhe'd breed ſtrife 'twixt me and my Wife,
And that all my Friends wou'd lead me a ſad Life;
Then Satan likewiſe did join each ſurmiſe,
And made me an helliſh Contrivance deviſe.

I promis'd her fair that I wou'd take Care
Of her and her Infant, and all Things prepare,
At *Hartlepool* Town, where ſhe ſhould lie down,
Poor Soul, ſhe believ'd me, as always ſhe'd done.

Thus wickedly bent, with her then I went,
She little expecting my bloody Intent;
We then drank ſome Ale, and I did prevail
With her to walk out, which ſhe did without fail.

We then took our Way to the Brink of the Sea,
And there like a Fury to her I did ſay,
You impudent Whore, that covets my ſtore,
I'm fully reſolv'd you ſhall plague me no more.

She dreading her Fate, alas! when too late,
Did call out for Mercy, whilſt I did her beat
With the Whip in my Hand, ſhe not able to ſtand,
Ran backwards and fell from the Rock to the Strand.

At this dreadful Fall, in Blood ſhe did ſprawl,
And had not the Power on Heaven to call;
And to blacken my Crime, the Babe which was mine,
I could percieve ſtirring within her ſome Time.

In hopes that the Sea would waſh her away,
I haſtened homewards without more delay:
But was taken ſoon, to have my ſad Doom,
And muſt periſh ſhamefully juſt in my Bloom.

Which makes my Heart ach, and ready to break,
I pray, my dear Saviour, ſome pity now take,
On Sinners the worſt, lewd, bloody, and curſt,
Who owns his Damnation both righteous and juſt.

But, Oh! my God, why ſhould my Saviour die,
If not to ſave Sinners as heinous as I:
Then come Cart and Rope, both ſtrangle and choak,
For in my Redeemer I ſtill truſt and hope.

Let all Men beware when married they are,
Lewd Women are ſurely a dangerous Snare;
Then Love your own Wives, thoſe Men only thrives,
That are the moſt pious and chaſte in their Lives.

F I N I S.

TIME FOR A RHYME

Good Lord! I'm undone, thy Face I would shun,
I've anger'd my God, and displeased his Son:
I dare not come nigh thy great Majesty,
Oh! where shall I hide my poor Soul when I die.

Thy Vengeance I dread on my guilty Head,
All Hopes of thy Mercy from me now are fled;
My poor sinful Soul is filthy and foul,
And Terror and Horror in my Conscience roll.

The Shame of my Race, and Mankind's disgrace,
My Actions all over were wicked and base;
No Devil in Hell that from Glory fell,
Can now with my Blood-guilty Soul parallel.

Her Affections I drew, how could I embrue
My Hands in her Blood! Oh! my God, I do rue
The curst hellish Deed, I made her to bleed,
That never did wrong me in thought, word, or deed,

I us'd my whole art, 'till I stole her Heart,
And swore to befriend her, and still take her Part,
Thus being beguil'd, she soon prov'd with Child,
Which made her weep sorely, but I only smil'd.

With sighs and with groans, with tears and with moans
She utter'd such Plaints as would soften flint Stone;
Oh! where shall I hide my Shame oft she cry'd,
Dear Sir, take some pity, and for me provide.

I fear'd she'd breed strife 'twist me and my Wife,
And that all my Friends wou'd lead me a sad Life;
Then Satan likewise did join each surmise,
And made me an hellish Contrivance devise.

In lieu of believing I took to deceiving
I lured her to me across the North Sea
My wicked intent to set her to rent
Among doxies and Whores that threaten'd my stores
I'm fully resolv'd you shall plague me no more.

Let all Men beware when married they are,
Lewd Women are surely a dangerous Snare;
Then Love your own Wives, those Men only thrives,
That are the most pious and chaste in their Lives.

*

Minette is trying her best to keep pace with the here and now, haunted by the memories of the morning. JoJo pulls her gently out of sight, away from the bar as she collapses against him. He longs to get her laughing once more, and tries an observation of the obvious. "The kid stinks worse than rotting fish!"

Instead of the hoped for smile, Minette gives way to her sobs. It's hard to make out the words, but at last JoJo understands that Claudine is dead. With no other choice, Minette has brought the baby to work.

"What else could I do, JoJo? I don't know what else to do!"

"Shh, ma petite." He steps across to the bar for a serviette and wipes her tears. "We'll fix this together." He turns around. "Nom de Dieu!"

A silk-coated gentleman is vomiting at the base of the bar. His guts on the floor, he grabs an orange from the crystal dish and staggers off. "For fuck's sake!" says JoJo, and immediately apologises. She shrugs, bad language the least of her problems. He swipes the red incendie bucket from its hook on the far wall. It's filled with sand as a safety requirement for fire emergencies, but handy as well for this clean-up.

Minette helps him spread out scoops of the absorbent stuff. "Take more than sand to hide this snootful!" She breathes out a small laugh. Stronger than she looks, thinks JoJo.

"I'll get the cleaner," he agrees. He's full of admiration for the recovery of her composure, and even more determined to help. "Quel bordel!" he says with good humour, and Minette returns his smile. He smooths the ruffled fringe from her forehead. "Sure you're all right?"

She nods, turning to attend the wailing infant. "Oui, mais la bébé ..."

JoJo reminds her there's a nurse backstage during the show, another safety precaution; he'll send her up. There's so much he wants to tell her, to ask her. But the show must go on and so must he. Laid out on the bar as decoration are some bouquets and sprays of blossom. He hands her a fragrant sprig to pin to her dress. A feeble attempt to hide the residual smell, but a kind gesture nonetheless.

Minette promises to watch the derring-do of the green-booted Troupe, enjoying his smile when she declares they're her favourite act. He leaves amid the baby's cries, and she remembers her mother's sure-fire remedy. Cuddling the little one against her, she rubs some brandy across its gums with her forefinger. Not everyone can afford Godfrey's Cordial from England.

*

HISTORY, NO MYSTERY IN A THICKENED PLOT

There were rats along the wharves of the Thames even before the Romans pitched their conquering camps. And rats still scamper every night along the tar-coated ship ropes in and out of grain stores, sniffling and snuffling noses toward the waxy wheels of French cheese awaiting market bids in the morning.

It's called The Age of Sail, has been for three hundred years. Little wonder The Gentleman is so at home around water. Born on the Isle of Dogs, he could swim before he could walk and knows every cobble as if he'd sculpted 'em himself. Waves of memory lap against the surface, flowing back and forth like a tidal river. Through the fog of bitter ale or stone cold sober, he can revisit familiar alleys, the rough touch of hessian, a campfire's flicker.

Each street marks out the gang boundaries. Little boys never get a choice; they acquire membership as soon as they slide from the womb. Baby girls grow to be the property of the gang, to use, abuse and trade as required. They get twisted into the fleshy shapes the boys hear about in pub songs, however painful, however humiliating. "Does she go downstairs, does she? Can you take her up the Chocolate Passage? Has she got a sister, mister?"

His gang is known as The Dirty Dogs. "Are you proud to be a Dirty Dog, son?" And the scrappy kid nods his head. "Can't hear ya'!" "Yessir!" He learns their rules like a catechism, their own brand of religion.

Nowadays, it's only on certain occasions that the Gentleman visits his chain of warehouses, barge moorings, and anchor rooms where he began as a trainee rat-catcher all those years ago. "Well I'll be a Dutchman!" he exclaims on his climb up the ladder of opportunity. Primed to Dockside gossip, he learns the laws of the land, when to reach and when to breach.

There's a perilous freedom on the Isle. Among a brood of tots that die or thrive, even his mother doesn't miss him back at home. Hidden away near the shore he stows a useful rowing boat, stolen right enough. A lad's prank and the canny way to establish his own patrol along Woolwich Docks. Back a bit from the river he can hunker down in the marsh grass to spy on the fortified naval base. Here in the safety of fantasy, he pretends to control the entire fleet of empire.

Woolwich gossip from over the water carries the buzz of armies being roused from the torpor of peace. Oh, there are plenty of excuses for war, most to do with palace egos and the easy profits collected by gouty-legged men of business. Testing ordnance to secure the progress of the nation... that's a favourite. The propaganda's all about safe and strong, but The Gentleman grows ever wary of deceit and weary of coffins filled with patriotism. For now, keep an eye peeled for those rats!

The latest enemies are Huns, though now you have to call 'em Prussians. Ignorant armies clashing by night. And day. Hard to fathom those Continentals. Far better to stop with Johnny Bulldog. His own kind, his own lingo. He's come quite a long way since then. It's all import-export now. You've already heard his catchy ballad by way of explanation.

But would he actually knock the door of recruitment, commit to a uniform and the threat to life and limb? Is he tempted to tag along, play dress-up with medals and braid, shoulder a musket and stab bayonet blades into sacks of straw?

Not on your Nelly Duff! Oh, yes, such a bright lad knows better than to befriend the weapons of war. That could get you killed stone dead, and then where would you be? In no fit state to get out of bed! A grave matter and no mistake. Hang low and let the rats laugh at his meagre jokes. Catching 'em is a daily test: keep a cool head, make a mental map, learn the lay of the land.

Long ago, his gaffer showed him the ropes and taught him how to knot 'em and untie 'em, too. Not only does he wake up alive, over the years he acquires a reputation. As so often with the way of things, this one tells that one and he tells another of a canny kiddie making a home in warehouse nooks and corners. When the gaffer's dodgy legs get the better of him, he bequeaths the territory to the boy. No snooty lawyers required, just a spit and a handshake. By then, of course, he's grown into a rangy young man.

As storage warehouses burn down and are rebuilt for the expanding trade with the world and his wife, it becomes obvious the rodents are winning the grain war. Such a filthy, smelly occupation, he muses... no prospects for betterment, not to mention refinement. He's getting rather keen on refinement.

The Gentleman learns such a lot keeping his peepers peeled. Knows which fires are innocent accidents... a lantern kicked over by chance, a pipe match dropped into the straw. And which insurance companies might be bribed to turn a blind eye away from arson. For a price. A going rate. Enough to splash out on a nightly pint, a pair of moleskin gloves, and a treat for his mates. Getting to be quite the gent, if you catch my drift.

But blackmail drips with danger. His gaffer says lie down with dogs, get up with fleas. And scarper when the dogs start the chase. "Are you a Dirty Dog?" "Yessir!" He fancies a clean uniform, and there's as decent a way to get one as anyone can contrive. It's right in the path of opportunity. Told you he's a bright lad.

A London mudlark helping out the Frenchies. Musing, distracted in his seat at the Folies, he takes himself back nearly twenty years, when his life turns a better corner.

On one of his self-appointed spy missions he learns the Woolwich garrison is to accept help from a battalion of Missouri Yanks shipped over from America. They'll need some tending, he thinks. He wants to get in on that action.

*

EMPIRE BUILDING WITHOUT A BULLET FIRED

It's the rich what gets the pleasure, so they say, and the poor what gets the blame. Still true today. Thinking the woman at the bar of the Folies-Bergère to be wild Claudine is The Gentleman's way of cleansing his soul. The temptation's just too strong to resist. For the French girl is the Eden snake, she loves it really. Downing all the drinks on offer, lifting her skirts above her knees to step onto a boatful of whores, being sick over the side on the Channel crossing, pinching their cheeks to revive the illusion of health... and all to satisfy the sex-starved red-necks billeted in a Woolwich warehouse.

His take of the profits turns him into a well-turned out young gent. But pimping ain't the occupation for the future. By a quirk of mistaken identity, he's given charge of some warehousing fit for the team of drays pulling a range of military vehicles. Horses are all well and good, but there's no appeal in a manure-filled career. Instead, he develops an affinity for all modes of transport, anything that moves over land and sea.

By the time the Huns have won across the water, Woolwich retains the thanks of the monarch. Never mind the battles' outcomes or the corpses left to rot in foreign fields; as the poet says, "Play up! play up! and play the game!" Its arsenals and parade grounds receive plenty of royal pennies to establish a solid naval base for decades to come.

New conflicts flare up and die with treaty signings. It's all one to those who wield the quill. Lads who play at soldiers along the river are finding easier ways to avoid the mud of actual armies. His network of spying and gossip proves the Gentleman's own observations that the number of drivers is dwindling. He knows they're important, drivers. Very important. Prototype tanks, lumbering across rough ground. Mobile kitchen units and even privies. But most of all it's the ambulance drivers that are saving the day. And they're so groomed, so well washed, well spoken. So respectable.

No one questions his appearance on the parade ground, nor does anyone acknowledge his part in the wild surmise of their orgies. Though he wears no uniform, they return his salute.

"Ever been to Burma?"

"Yessir!" He's never been out of the Stratford Borough.

"Think you can handle an ambulance, sonny me lad?"

"Yessir!"

"Ever driven a vehicle before?"

"Yessir!" Though he hasn't a clue.

"Right you are," says the Petty Officer second class. He hands over the motor winder. "Take it for a turn."

The young Gentleman climbs into the van, releasing the brake. He manages to steer in a straight line to the edge of the grounds, but crashes into a perimeter wall. Just a small dent, lucky him, no great damage. Somehow his confidence carries him down and he meets the officer head on.

"Never mind," he says. "You're hired. We move out tomorrow."

"Yessir!"

"This time next week you'll be swimming in the Irrawaddy." Whatever that is!

I can't promise and nor can he, that he might indulge in a bout of pimping, just to help out his pals, you understand. But he's now a respectable Gentleman. See for yourself.

*

WHAT THEY GET UP TO ACROSS THE CHANNEL

The cleaner arrives with a pail of carbolic acid dissolved in water, losing no time to scrub away at the pile of smothered vomit. Meanwhile, Minette prepares the baby in her cot, and hands it to the protection of the nurse, her mind at rest.

Glad to be of help, nevertheless the nurse catches her breath. "That carbolic's a bit sharp! Make your eyes water!" Minette and the cleaner join her soft laughter. "Wait... I know!" She offers an unexpected tip, suggesting they peel some of the oranges and rub the bar and the floor beneath with their oily zest. As she leaves them she says, "Never fear, she'll be safe with me downstairs."

At last, with the lull before the storm of the show, Minette has a moment of peace to review the galloping deeds of the day, to let her grief take the reins. She fingers the amulet hanging from the velvet ribbon around her neck. Claudie always insisted she wear it in her stead. "He give it me, Min. He's bound to come back some day, and he'll spot it, for sure."

They have no secrets, the sisters. Never did, even as kiddies. One knew when the other had dropped a mitten in the snow, or hid Maman's spectacles out of spite. So when reckless Claudie recounts what the Gentleman expects of her, the unusual positions, the sharing with other men, other women, Minette sees past the simple recitation to her sister's inner pain. "He's got a bulge along his nose, and one of his ears is all bashed up. Says that brooch is his mum's."

Not bloody likely, thinks Minette. It all washes out with her tears as she stands and waits. Claudie's death. The unfortunate child.

She catches the shadow of an approaching customer, greeting him by rote without looking up. "Something to drink, m'sieur?"

"Gimme a Bass," says the Gentleman, pointing to the ale bottle with its red triangle on the label. He's checking the crowd and barely sees her.

Minette raises her eyes to him, then quickly lowers her gaze. He fits Claudine's description exactly. Just then, the orchestra calls attention with a long drum-roll and clash of cymbals. JoJo and the green boots are about to perform one of their most daring feats of balance.

*

ONCE A PIMP...

The Gentleman says, "Well, well, if it ain't Zazie Cocotte." Drink slurs his words. "Been looking for you, you minx."

Minette clicks the top off the beer bottle, sliding it toward the man who's leering at her, the man who betrayed her sister. She clutches at the amulet. "Wearing your bauble, I see." He tries to reach over the bar to touch her neck, but she blocks his arm with another bottle.

She looks up, hoping to catch JoJo's eye. He sees her and nods. He knows there's no time to navigate the tunnel under the stage and get up to the loge bar in time to confront the Gentleman. Must be another way. He channels his rage into calm ingenuity.

JoJo sees the man lurch around the bar and lay his hands on Minette's shoulders. She averts her head as the Gentleman whispers, "Time for another sail across the Channel." Spittle sprays onto his moustache.

Which is when JoJo signals to the orchestra. Another extended drum-roll turns every head up to the heights of the trapeze.

The Troupe swings from opposite ends of the stage, turning, twisting, grabbing each other by the wrists and settling down to balance on platforms.

*

A TRULY GRAND FINALE

While the audience is diverted by their antic skill, JoJo flips the magnetic board, the gift from Mam'selle Aimée, the Human Fly.

It dangles unsupported at the far end, hovering high above the upturned faces of the crowd. They gasp. What is the great JoJo going to do now? Surely he cannot walk out to such danger. And what's that contraption strapped around his waist?

Minette is trapped by the bulk of the Gentleman pressing against her. She can just see past his shoulder to JoJo on the level above her. He signals to the orchestra to stop playing. Silence settles the house. Then, with the suddenness of a miracle, JoJo steps upside down onto the dangling board.

The audience gasps. They cannot believe their eyes. The Gentleman finally looks up, as mesmerised as everyone else. He drops his hold on Minette. Step by careful step the acrobat walks out to the end of the board. Upside down. Without a net. Even his most loyal fans have never seen him attempt such daring. First one, then another, and soon the entire audience begins clapping a steady rhythm to accompany his aerial journey.

He's still about a third of the way to the upper alcove and has reached the end of the board. The clapping fades away as JoJo flips himself upright and releases the thick rope around his middle. He flings it over the polished balustrade of the loge. It's attached to a rock climber's grappling hook. JoJo tugs the rope, testing for slack. It's taut and catches solidly. No one dares breathe.

With the precision of a jungle gibbon he runs across the makeshift tightrope, leaping onto the startled Gentleman, knocking him to the floor. No one treats JoJo's lady love with such disrespect.

The orchestra strikes up a jolly tune. Aha! As one, the audience exhales. It's all part of the act. They erupt into cheers and applause and whistles. For years to come they speak of this night, how they witnessed a miracle, how they got their money's worth and no mistake. Sometimes the legend of the show overtakes the truth.

*

WALKING ON AIR

Within the year Minette and JoJo declare their vows. They have entwined their love around Claudie's baby, raising her as their own, passing on her name. On this day of their wedding ceremony, Minette has made the little one a robe embroidered all over with rose buds. Smiling beneath the delicate lace of her bridal veil, she becomes Madame Joseph.

The entire event, given the precision of all his presentations, is arranged by Monsieur Sarin... tasteful, full of joy, in the modest chapel of Rue de Bac. It's that venue, the alleged site of the miracle of the Virgin, that can appease the fans who continue to celebrate the miracle of the tightrope. And, it must be said, the persistent legend still boosts ticket sales. Canny Monsieur Sarin, smiling on the crowds who wait outside to shower the beaming couple with tiny squares of coloured confetti and petals of primrose.

Et maintenant, after the wedding feast of succulent meats and buns washed down with a special vintage and all the cast invited to be sure... JoJo and his bride are off across the Atlantic. A working honeymoon with baby in tow. Vaudeville performances are already announced to eager crowds, illustrations of handmade costumes designed by Madame Minette herself. And, shh! Time for secret appointments with a certain Florenz Ziegfeld Jr, discussions aimed at managerial representation throughout the United States of America. And perhaps a contract to record moving images of their show. The cinema devised by the Lumière brothers of France is proving quite the fascination for tractor drivers, factory girls, and the upper crust right the way across the new world. JoJo's Troupe is to be filmed in New York studios and far away in a small town in the orange groves of California.

This is the legacy of the Folies-Bergère, ladies and gents. We hope you have enjoyed the show.

***

KWICKIE KAPTION 2

Although this fragment of a 4th century AD Roman mosaic from a Sicilian villa is frequently referred to as the room of the ten dancing girls, it actually depicts women engaged in various sporting a ctivities, including lifting weights and indoor ball games. They wear the two-piece bikini tops and bottoms that wouldn't be out of place in female changing rooms today. The Romans adapted the garments over several centuries from Grecian sportswear.

It's not my idea of a wonder bra...

whatever happened to lift and separate?!

CHAPTER FOUR – A HARD PLACE

Petite fille dans un fauteuil bleu **1878 Mary Cassatt**

Born in Pennsylvania in 1844, Mary Cassatt was one of the pioneers of Impressionism. Living most of her life among like-minded artists in France, one of her most enduring friendships was with her mentor Edgar Degas. There is much controversary about how intimate their relationship may have been, but they both yearned for the freedom to paint whatever they chose and in any style they chose. The little dog in the picture was a favourite of Cassatt, and had been a gift from Degas.

She remained single to her death in 1926, leaving a legacy of portraits and studies of women behind closed doors.

My story focuses on the child in the painting titled Little Girl in a Blue Armchair. It's told around and about her, mixing memories and family histories, all concerned with aspects of power and edging toward a dark resolution.

A Hard Place

Echoes, loud and bruising:

Nanny Todd, lock that vile child in her room. And. I hate you! You're not my real mother! And. Get that flea-ridden dog out of my house!

When Papa brought his new bride home from the wedding she remembered her manners, smiled and held out her hand. "Hello," soft-voiced, "I'm Vivi."

"What kind of name is that, child? John, what is her name?"

"Violet. After her mother."

[Echoes. Barely heard.]

From the first, she'd taken against The Woman, but had tried to behave for Nanny Todd's sake. She hardly remembered her own mother and couldn't fully comprehend why she'd gone away or why she couldn't come back to them. Young as she was, Vivi assumed she'd done something wrong, but didn't know what that might be. Then Papa said Nanny Todd would be looking after her, which was fine. In no time she'd been won over by this smiley woman, round as a dumpling and always ready with a hug and a sweet biscuit when the occasion demanded.

Strictly speaking The Woman was still in mourning, her marriage to Vivi's Papa celebrated in haste. Under her black veil her complexion greyed. She tried to suppress a bubbling of bile rising in her throat. As the doctor had warned her. "Show me to my rooms, please."

Vivi's hand remained outstretched. Unshaken.

“Of course, my dear. You must be fatigued from the journey.” It was no more than five miles, but in her defense, there were circumstances.

Papa bent down and whispered, “I’ll tell you a secret. You'll have a baby brother after a while. Or sister. Won’t that be nice?”

Vivi was very good at keeping secrets.

*

Papa was John, never any nicknames, and The Woman always insisted on being addressed formally as Adeline, [which she knew to mean of noble birth]. She gave short shrift to anyone who tried to diminish her as Ada [so common] or Alita, [which didn’t even sound American].

If truth could squeeze in however, her name was actually Cora. She’d come up in the world from the Appalachia of her unremarkable, even humble family heritage of hand-me-downs and the dismissal of those busy keeping up with the Joneses. Once, perhaps, regarded as ‘salt of the earth,’ such ‘soldiers of the soil’ were more to be pitied than censured, if they were thought of at all. Later of course, more affluent Others had no reason to doubt her, all trace of Mountain Folk long drowned in the creeks of her childhood.

Adeline acquired a selection of lace gloves along with her hauteur as a vital part of her new role in life. By the time she’d ingratiated herself into the political circles of influence, the gloves hid any residual callouses, and she’d long ago learned never to refer to those rivers as ‘cricks.’ That just wouldn’t do for the wife of a Senator.

In her estimation, propriety trumped politics. She was perfectly capable of understanding the nuances of power-grabs, but found it easy to blink away from rule-breaking when her own position was threatened. Any threat to her husband was just as precarious. Her motivation was never loyalty nor affection, but very much a matter of status. Ladder climbing her new profession. Perhaps her greatest asset was the patience to listen. Listen and learn. Over the years she'd stored such secrets to protect them both.

Having been raised as the third eldest of ten, all canny with mud-crusted toes, young Cora knew the significance of her mother's constant pregnancies. By the time she'd transformed herself into Adeline and allowed the Senator to mount her like a field pony, she knew just how to jeopardise the predictable fetus. And, when it was extracted, lifeless, from her, how to display her pretense at grief, along with the ambiguity of blame against him. After that, the Senator had to seek out paid bodies to salve his sense of guilt amid dwindling lust.

"Such a shame," agreed his constituents with genuine concern, "that they haven't been blessed with children."

Don't ever presume, Adeline often reminded herself, to know what goes on behind closed doors.

*

Her late husband's physical decline emboldened her to expect unquestioned obedience from her staff; his position in state politics reinforced her sense of entitlement. As the Senator's wife, she'd organized their domestic life into as viable a business as his matters of state, played hostess at elaborate supper parties, and had become familiar with the culinary tastes of his associates, if not always their post-prandial predilections. Skeletons? Oh, she knew which closets contained most of them.

Adeline left all the funeral arrangements to the frock-coated Director, spending most of the ceremony wondering where she might order the thick silk band around his top hat. Once the casket had been interred, she pinned back her black face veil and prepared to greet those intimates invited to the gathering in the state drawing room.

Only the cathedral-high ceiling provided enough space to down-play the overall atmosphere of dried blood red from the walls, carpet and matching curtains. The irony was not lost on her, considering the fatal thrusts and parries by a century of ruthless, ambitious politicos.

It was a room she knew she'd have to vacate; she'd already strangled any emotional attachment to the décor and furniture. The carriage clock on the stone mantel, the tear-shaped leaves of glass on the matching chandeliers, golden legs supporting the marble sideboard, portraits of people she didn't know. She kept an eye on the hired-in catering staff, offering trays of funerary nourishment. Smiling modestly at the women, she eyed up the men as though they were auditioning for a new role. Which, in fact, they were.

John wasn't a political colleague. In fact, Adeline wasn't entirely sure what his connection was to her late husband, something to do with providing financial advice, she thought. His regular features and natty outfit proved a good start for further discovery. She was particularly attracted by the deep dimple of his chin; she could imagine tracing it lightly with her forefinger. When he revealed he, too, had recently lost his wife to illness, Adeline turned her full attention to their promising acquaintance.

But when John suggested – as was the usual custom and practice - melting down some of the Senator's gold fobs and cuff links to fashion commemorative rings and distribute them to the mourners, she contrived a way to refuse without revealing what an abhorrent idea she considered it. Besides, she had far more imaginative plans for her inheritance.

*

As for John, despite enjoying his late wife's inherited wealth, it had been a love match. At the beginning. Before he simply grew away from her. Captivated at first by her inviting smile and tantalising cleavage, he hadn't realised just how boring she actually was. They'd been so full of plans during the courtship, and the extravagance of their nuptials became known locally as 'the wedding of the century.' He looked forward to showing her off to the world on their year-long honeymoon.

Little by little she'd eroded his enthusiasm. Amused by the silly faces of the camels at the Pyramids at Giza, she refused to join him for a ride. She begrudged the waste of money when he tossed a handful of coins into the Trevi Fountain. But she brightened at the sight of their deluxe suite in the Pavillon de la Reine. Not the grandest, to be sure, but all that marble and glass inspired her to plan a complete redecoration of their *pied-à-terre* back in America.

Their Paris jaunt proved more salacious than romantic, for it was only after extempore solo midnight visits to the whores of Pigalle that he was able to transfer the excitement to the marital bed.

Then, the inevitable. She announced her pregnancy as they strolled through the wide plaza beneath the legs of the Eiffel Tower. He wasn't elated by the news, but diverted her attention to the view overhead: so solid steel, contrived to represent lightness, freedom. Staring upward confused her, made her feel faint.

Back in the hotel, she wanted the curtains drawn, blocking the city from view. They might as well be anywhere. He couldn't even indulge in the nightly creations of the chef as she cried off from supper in the grand salon. He tried to offer her support, but there were only so many tisane and dry toast meals he could stomach.

They left for home earlier than planned. A mutual decision. He fabricated a telegram calling him back on a business deal. She wanted the comfort of her own doctor to monitor the ripening melon inside her. With unhidden joy, she placed his hand on her honeymoon belly. It revolted him. And so the months passed.

Parisian prostitutes were thin on the ground back home. Oh, he could find them, but he couldn't risk scandal on his home territory. Such frustration. In the end it was all about the money. As so many women do, she died soon after the birth. No one had a name for what killed her; the accepted term was ‘complications.’ He preserved his reputation, extending his mourning. But he knew in his heart it was all about the money. And, of course, little Vivi.

*

But, as the poets say, time’s winged chariot rolled on apace. John easily succumbed to Adeline’s determination. Their marital union set tongues wagging throughout the county. Who was besting whom? The money met in the middle. The widow’s inheritance equal to the widower’s. Well-suited in that sense. Whenever they appeared together in public, her gloved hand rested lightly on his forearm, their steps matched; never a coiffed curl out of place, nor a bowtie askew.

*

The inevitable once again. At least this time his wife’s condition wasn’t decorated with illusions of happy families growing ever closer with the swell of her middle. Strict adherence to social etiquette demanded a protracted period of confinement. As with so many customs, this one harked back to medieval England. A pre-birth ritual trapped a pregnant woman in her bed-chamber, however luxurious, attended by caring relatives and midwives to assure the safe arrival of the baby. Contemporary Edwardian practice now recommended at least another month of enforced rest for the health of mother and child. And more progressive practitioners reckoned it was vital for something they referred to as bonding between the pair.

True to form, however, Adeline proved no slave to convention and continued her schedule of visits to charity asylums and to the launch of new consumer emporiums in neighbouring states. The latter taking precedence over the former. Far more intriguing and far fewer judgmental stares. After all, the imminent baby was destined to be handed over to others to rear, while the latest fashions from overseas would last at least for a season or two.

John welcomed Adeline’s frequent absences, his revulsion at her full belly as potent as at his first wife’s. And it allowed him more time with Vivi. Such a devoted father. From the first, Nanny Todd had always been given a free half-day and full Sunday to spend time with her own family.

*

Once Adeline was helped into her carriage, and Nanny had set off on foot down the tree-lined drive, Vivi knew it was time to wait, sprawled out on one of the plush blue armchairs in the lounge. She arranged herself. Dress awry revealing bare legs. No need to disturb the dog; it would sleep straight through.

As requested, before leaving that morning Nanny Todd had dressed her charge in the brand new lace outfit The Woman had brought back from her latest shopping trip. It came complete with Scotch plaid shawl and matching socks. There was a tartan soldier's cap, too, but that wasn't for indoors.

*

Neither she nor her Papa stopped to question the rights and wrongs. This was just what happened. Urgency replaced by habit. A matter of power. Invitation in bright eyes and a smile of expectation. Just an echo of Pigalle.

Did The Woman know? Did she suspect? There was no longer any need for Papa to whisper in his daughter's ear. Vivi was very good at keeping secrets.

***

CHAPTER FIVE – THE GHOST GOOSE

A Woman Walking In A Farm aka Woman With A Goose 1902

Pauline Modersohn-Becker

Too often overlooked as an artist of conviction and innovation, Paula Modersohn-Becker's output was prolific. Sadly it was also overshadowed by the work of her husband Otto, and her close friendship with poet Rainer Maria Rilke and their Boho colleagues, some of whose portraits she displayed.

Born in Dresden in 1876, she died tragically of an embolism at the age of 31 in Bremen, having recently giving birth to her first child. Using both impressionist and expressionist techniques, her work celebrated the everyday life of the working class, and provided an honest and uncensored depiction of mothers and children. She was the first woman artist in the world to have a museum named in her honour.

The painting that inspired my story has no official title, but is known as Woman With A Goose, and A Woman Walking In A Farm. I've tried to create her entire life from that single image

THE GHOST GOOSE

SECTION ONE – A Little Girl

Once upon a time there was a farm. You would have to look very hard to tell it was a farm, because it looked exactly like the shapeless patch of mud and wilderness that surrounded it. When the sun decided to shine upon the land, it always passed right by the farm, heading for pastures where the grass was greener. You would have to look very hard to spot many green blades on this farm.

And yet, the ground gave up its rootlings, potatoes and carrots and purple-skinned rutabagas. A few cabbages left by the grubs and slugs. Yes, the farm was tended by a farmer. Now well past her prime, she'd managed the land on her own ever since she was a little girl, when an implacable funnel of swirling dust picked up her parents by the scruff of their necks and whirled them away.

On that day - so long ago she could just see it in the corner of her eye, waving through the undergrowth - the little girl had been playing in the cow shed next to the farmhouse. Yes, there was a farmhouse, once, and yes, there was a shed - rough and ready but serviceable enough for beasts and their sucklers, shelves to store tools and provisions, and a worktable. An adjacent stone silo dried out the green mix of barley and kale, sileage to feed the cattle over the winter.

To be frank, there was only one cow in the unheated shed, held safe between roughly sawn timber braces. The little girl took warmth from the kind breath of the beast. They lived too far from the town for friends; school only ever a dream. She was content, used to being on her own, devising games from the tools and tufts around her. When she was just learning to walk, her mother would sit her on a mound of straw with a pile of stones and a hand-made wicker basket, woven from the willow that framed the well spring. The baby found great amusement in dropping each stone into the basket and taking them all out again. Later, tickling the succession of barn kittens always brought a smile; their comic antics preparing them to make enemies of the determined harvest mice.

She was a welcome little bundle to be sure, but quite a surprise for her parents. She'd come to them late in their lives together, and they were careful not to scare her away.

Neither priest, physician nor prophet pulled at the baby's birth, but the couple had learned from their cattle to cut the cord and clear the caul from her nose. They named her Charlotte. It was a name that floated in the public air, the name of a princess. Or was it a queen? From the first, her mother called her Lottie. Other people called her mother Missus, and they called her Little Missy. To her father she was always 'My goodly goosie.' And he was known as Mister, whether they respected him or not. Who could tell?

The cow never minded what anyone's name was. It was the sniff of them that mattered, the truth of their caress. Her father showed Lottie how to put the new-born calf up to the udders, and taught her to tug them, gentle and firm so the milk would come. Some for the calf, some for the bucket. The tried and tested technique he'd learned as a little boy.

Once, as she showed her father that she too had mastered the technique, the cow gave forth a mighty fart. She shrieked and jumped off the milking stool, so startled that the cow kicked over the pail. What a tribute to her father's patience and good humour that he began to laugh, a bubble of mirth escaping his mouth and growing into a roar. It soothed the cow and calmed his daughter. He perched her on his knee as he explained about gassy emissions from beast and man alike.

Her father claimed the cow shed as his domain; the kitchen was his wife's. Lottie found comfort in both worlds, like a fish which could walk or a flying giraffe. When the milk pail was almost full, he'd inspect the level and hand it back to her. "Here, my goodly goosie girl, this is for your mother."

And she would bob her head. "I will not nor never spill a drop." She clamped the handle tight, balanced it close to her body, each step taken on alien ground, no assumptions, until she reached the farmhouse. The door already ajar for her delivery, she knew how to step over the threshold. Her mother chuckled at the whoosh of relief as she set the pail onto the table. The milk slipped up one side, threatened the rim just a little, then settled into the whole. A dragon conquered - another challenge met, another claim to her heritage.

Visitors were few and far between, as the saying goes. The little girl learned who might be trusted and whom to blow away like cuckoo spit. There was no one to ask about this or that. No one on hand as baby Lottie kicked off the blanket her mother had knitted and stepped away from her milky bosom, growing fast into the calm, curious child the parents both adored. Neither granny's ghost nor the fabled witches three imparted wisdom, yet they muddled along, learning as they went. The mother, the father, the little girl. Ma, Pa, and Lottie.

The couple regaled her with the peek-a-boo game. "Eyes," they chanted. And "eyes," she said. They touched the chimney breast, pointed at hens, and petals. Looking to the sky, they named clouds and colours, the changing faces of the moon... whatever came into view. "Show me your knees, Lottie." And she would. "Where is the cake, Lottie." With her eyes atwinkle, she pushed the half-chewed confection onto her lower lip, and the three of them laughed so hard the crumbs spattered all over the table. By the time she could jabber away and make any sense, she'd learned to count on her fingers and toes. True enough the couple had no books and neither could barely sound out the words to read. But they lullabied their baby to sleep and filled her toddler head with folk tales relayed through the ages. With such ad hoc instruction, Lottie discovered her world.

And here I will tell you something gratis and for free about Education. Trace it to the Latin *educare*. Leading out. Out of ignorance? Of Eden's Garden? Out of sight, but not out of mind. If only they'd known.

Lottie grew into a reasonable replica of her mother, though not yet so broad in the beam, as they say. No one, beloved or a stranger, ever mistook her for pretty - her squat neck balanced too near her chest, her small nose, like the father's, a bit too sharp. Looks were the least of it. But she listened, and watched, and learned. Her smile lit up shadows of doubt. Fear was never her style. She had all the confidence of a cocky crow at harvest, which certainly helped smooth the transitions from seasons of bounty to piercing the icy crusts down in the well.

The girl rubbed her hands over the cow's sweet face and breathed in her smell. She'd seen that cow seeded and born, helped her parents bring it to size. She stood between them in the yard when the butcher boy's cart arrived, drawn by two yoked shire horses with their furry feet, strong as oxen, bumping across the bland hills up to the shed. The bull stood the journey, haunches taut with anticipation and resignation.

"Morning, Mister," greeted the butcher's boy. "Morning, Missus, morning, Little Missy."

"Morning, Deet," they replied.

He'd brought the butcher's best bull, rented out to keep every cow in calf. His father owned the abattoir, too, the only one for miles, but near enough to save the animals from panic. Relaxed. Better for the meat. Many a small herd willingly walked to their ultimate journey over the hills and up from the dells accompanied by a flute and tune from the drovers. The men swished long withy stems against the flanks of the slow movers. They'd learned their songs from their own fathers and grand-fathers, from the faded days when the better-off farmers sat atop tooled leather yelling ti-yi-yip all the way to market. Leagues and leagues away.

Feet in the stirrups and seat in the saddle,
We hung and rattled with them long-horn cattle.

But listen more closely when they were full up to the knocker with ale and sailor's rum; listen then to those songs of kine and bullock. Then they bragged of bare bottoms and unruly members, flaccid themselves and helpless with laughter at their bawdry. The hired slaughtermen took it all in their stride. Old tunes, even older themes.

The butcher himself was always looking out ways to improve, be it replacing equipment or learning the latest in husbandry from regional journals and cattle auction gossip. He ran the shop in town and his wife looked after the market stall with Deet. She was blessed with rosy cheeks that looked painted on, giving her a hint of modesty. His bushy brows nearly met across the bridge of his nose, scary at first glance, but his hearty laugh forged friendships with everyone.

They lived in a big house down the lane at the end of the High Road, the abattoir just out of hearing. They worked round the clock, protecting their promise to raise prime animals from calf to table roast. Yet there was still time to parade the best of them to compete for medals at the local show. Even as a toddler, Deet had already been awarded rosettes for his heifers.

The auctions, of course, were a much more serious proposition, setting price standards for the year to come. If you sliced up sawney rashers, beef, or lamb on your platter, it was sure to have passed through the butcher's hands one way or another. His name was Bert Filey, and yes, some called him Butcher Bertie, but no wonder most folk knew him as the Meat Master.

Led from the cart by its nose ring and into the field, Filey's best bull knew what to do. After all, it had covered most of the cattle grazing beneath the mountains on the horizon. 'Tis common to walk when prize beasts do ride. Lottie's parents encouraged her to watch the mounting, urgent and frightening, and allowed her to calm the cow afterward, stroking her nose, scratching her forehead.

Months later, when it was time for the calving, the little girl got her first birth blooding. This wee beast for the slaughter, next year's for raising. The couple kept on their matching marriage rings, now too tight to remove, as they washed her hands with their own, colouring the clear water in the pail redder than red. "The devil himself has dipped in his tail," said her father.

*

She watched her mother make cakes and soft bread, rising to satisfaction inside the cast iron stove. The run-around ducks and chickens in the farmyard were never stingy with their eggs, which she cracked with a sharp snap against the edge of the table. She forked them into softened slabs of butter churned from the creamy foam of the milk, measured out handfuls of flour from the mill, and stirred it all together, sweetened with her store of apple pulp. Into the baking tray it all went. Ever fed with chopped wood, the oven was always ready to receive, to work magic, to complete the transformation. She helped her mother tie her two middle fingers together with string.

"To remind me to take the cakes out," she told her daughter. "Else they burn to cinder and slag."

"And then we will not sell them," said Lottie. Her mother nodded with pride at the little one's wisdom.

The farm always needed tending to this or that, keeping the whole family busy for months till the cart returned. Lottie knew it would again be driven by Deet, the butcher's boy, come to take away the calf. Care and killing. Killing and care. No secrets here. She stood by the farmhouse, watching the path deliver him to full height, her stare bold upon him. He stole her in glimpses, catching the curl that escaped from her cap, the way she backed her rounded rump against the door frame. It would take another summer or two to act on his rising desire, till she was fully baked. Today he turned to loading the cart.

As they did every market day, her parents took pains to meet their neighbours with a wash and brush up. Mister hit his flat cap sharply against his knee; he always wore it to cover his bald spot. "Nonsense, my goosie girl," he joked to his daughter. "I've a full head of hair, look, falling down to my very knees!"

Lottie helped her mother pull off her cotton arm defenders before changing her house tunic for the fawn jacket that fastened with bone buttons. As Deet set off, they followed behind, taking turns to push the wobbly barrow, packed with her mother's hand-knitted scarves, her home-made cakes and loaves and jars of pickled cabbage, her father's wood-crafted chairs and carvings, and whatever dug-up roots they could spare. It was a long walk to town, but they were strong and trusted their legs. Young Lottie stood outside the farmhouse door to wave them all good-bye.

No, she was not allowed to come with them. She'd never felt the familiar dirt path harden underfoot into the cobbled High Road. Nor was she allowed to give the calf a name, to hug its neck and feel its rough tongue across her face. But none could stop her wondering whether Deet's taut haunches ever quivered and released like a prize bull.

The moon would be out by the time her parents returned, pulling the barrow of traded supplies. Parcels of peas and beans jostled with green-skinned apples, bruised where they'd fallen. Cool blocks of cheese wrapped in blanched nettle leaves. A handy handful of wooden plugs to fasten timber. Bags of green sileage. And jute sacksful of charcoal and kindling.

The Meat Master returned them veal neck or shank, perhaps some chops or short ribs, hooves to boil down for glue, tallow candles fashioned from kidney suet, and, as proof of purchase, the pair of ears. He kept the best cuts, of course, for sale at the shop and on the market stall. Well, that was the whole point, wasn't it? The selling, the buying. To live another day, another year.

Lottie helped unload, a place for everything and everything in its place, as the saying goes. Her father stacked his supplies alongside ripening fruit and dried legumes. "Pass me some of that tea, Lottie." She handed over one of the lidded canisters. She'd already learned the angular markings were actually Chinese letters, though no one could read the words they spelled. "A man needs a brew at his work bench," her father declared. And who would dare argue with that?

Whenever he wanted to, he could heat a pan on his small Primus stove. Her mother, kitchen-busy as ever, would simmer the apples, mash and smash and strain it all through squares of muslin; then she'd scoop the paste into a bowl, nature's sugar, and perfect for baking. None of them ever had trouble sleeping on market day. And the next morning…

When Lottie saw her mother lift down the glazed light-brown bowl, chipped along the rim, and rummage for her wooden mixing spoon, she knew she was in for a treat. As each cake found its place in the oven, she got to lick the thick streaks of batter. It filled her mouth like sweet, sweet mud.

Once, as a birthday surprise, the parents brought back a hank of yarn to transform into a playmate. Pa whittled out a tiny spoon, and Ma helped twist the yarn into a face. The little girl had been saving two black buttons, found in the field, and she sewed them onto the toy for eyes. One was bigger than the other, giving it an air of surprise. Then Ma ripped off the hem of her raggedy skirt and coaxed it into a new dress for her daughter. She helped her fashion the leftover shreds into clothes for the little doll. No one had told them how or why. They just got on with it and laughed at the novelty. The little girl watched and learned and, braver by the day, tried her hand at it all. Indoors and out. Outdoors and back in.

The months and years got churned into the ground, like ashes from the grate. Each dawn offered expectations, challenges. Each night, the refreshment of sleep. Mother, Father, and Little Girl.

Then, on that fateful afternoon, Lottie stood in the doorway, half in, half out, the sun warm on her back, her eyes on her parents. She kicked at some leaves that had blown inside, and saw her father help tie the bit of reminder string around her mother's fingers. He wiped the sweat from his forehead with the checked square of cloth round his neck; then he made a clicking noise in her direction and winked as he enclosed his wife in a generous embrace. Mister and Missus. Little Missy blushed at the intimacy. She smelled the cakes and loaves in the oven, baking to golden perfection. Chores of the morning all done, she sought a bit of fantasy from the steady boredom of the day.

It wasn't hot and it wasn't cold. She might have played among the rows of roots, but instead she'd escaped to the shed. Light seeped through gaps where the wooden siding overlapped. When she was younger, she imagined they were magic beams that fell from the roof, a pathway from fairyland. It was cooler inside, and the cowie lowed as she entered. Lottie spent some time with the beast, scratching the clump of hair between her ears.

Looking around for something to take her attention, soon she was balancing her elbows on the work bench as she drew faces on two tilling spades with bits of charcoal. She focused so intently, never noticing the sky had turned green nor the sudden silence. Crickets in the yard and the birds in the barley all ceased their songs. Her work was precise and took some time. Which was quite lucky for her, as it turned out, because whatever it was that took away her parents, also nudged the farmhouse off balance, lifted it like a lamb carcass ready for the butcher's blade, and dashed it to the ground.

The cow shed was only a few feet away, so Lottie clearly heard the sounds of destruction, though she couldn't tell what was happening. More cautious than frightened, she stayed where she was, putting her fingers to her lips to warn the spade-folk to keep quiet. By the time all the noise had found other places to be, she opened the shed door. The farm was gone. Most of the root crop rows had vanished into the pitted soil. Not a trace of the house, though not far from the path Lottie could see the spout of their kettle, half a chair, and something shiny but she couldn't tell what. Lottie knew the field workers only showed up on certain days. Today wasn't one of them.

Far off, forks of lightning burst above the hills of the horizon, followed by muffled thunder. Her mother had told her that the sound was 'the wee folk banging drums on the hilltop,' though she never explained who the 'wee folk' actually were. Where was her mother now? And where was her father? Were they lying hidden in a faraway field, injured and needing help? She called and called to them. But no one answered.

Well, that wasn't quite true. The more she shouted into the gloom, the stronger came the reply of a certain honking. A clunky kind of honk. Craggy-voiced and rumbling from the depths of a seed-filled crop, coughed up into the air with a throat full of feathers.

As Lottie walked across the land, she couldn't even guess why everything had simply disappeared. Matters of wind and weather could only be learned by direct experience, or second-hand tales. Of course, she'd felt rain, fragile flakes of snow, and all sorts of breeze and gale. She'd been told never to stare at the sun. "Folk go blind, my goodly goosie girl, just for a moment's dare." But no one had ever revealed more rare, selective events, like the eruption of a volcano, a meteor shower, or a sea wave that forced its way onto the land.

She'd never been beyond the beyond. Anyone she'd met had come to them - she had no idea from where. Neighbours and friends, the market, the town, and tales from the city, all of them indicated by her father with a wave of his arm in the general direction of 'over there.'

On that day of distress and disaster she was reaching toward her twelfth year, and had learned every task and trial on the farm. Dropping seed at just the right distance, stamping it in with a slosh of water taught her anticipation. She learned that green shoots would appear soon, but that soon was a concept, not an appointment. She'd helped the field hands with harvesting and knew which tit-bits the weaners liked best. A farmer in the making, her parents' pride and joy.

She still hadn't been allowed to accompany them to the market, but she was as strong and healthy as they and could walk for miles. If she ever got the chance. Once she trailed her father across the fields as he strode angrily to punish a fox that had massacred his hens. They came back empty-handed, though he praised her loyalty and stamina. Reward indeed!

Seeking out the missing parents was top of her list, but, young as she was, she knew she had to find something else: a way to survive in the midst of devastation. She cleared a rough and ready space in the cow shed, and swept away the debris underneath the eaves.

Some time ago her mother had acquired a sewing machine, run by a foot treadle, but after years of wear, it had broken. The belt was worn through, the balance wheel hand crank refused to engage, and the bobbin winder had snapped off. Though her father had pledged to mend it, there it sat, unused and sad under the work bench, covered with a woollen blanket that itself had seen better days. "Not to worry," said Ma. "I prefer knitting." Now it was the blanket that Lottie needed. Come bedtime, she plumped up a pile of straw into a soft nest and lay down next to the cow, covering herself with the ragged cloth. It smelled of dried oil, but kept her warm enough to sleep through the night.

Sometimes sleep just wouldn't come. Was it the intrusion of a full moon, or the rock pile of fresh ideas tumbling into her mind, each one dislodging another? She pulled on her rubber boots, careful not to wake the cow, and groped around to light the candle in Pa's storm lamp. She tried to sort shrubs from imaginary trolls as she searched the circle of illumination in the yard. At last her eyelids closed in sleep, and when she awoke it was daylight.

Without clock nor calendar, it was hard to say how much time had passed. Lottie measured seasons not days. Discovery became her occupation, her obsession. Every morning brought the nagging rasp of expectation. Determined to find her parents, she strode this way and that, as the birds fly, seeking direction in clues from the ground below. Besides, there was only one path out of the farm and only one way back.

The more she examined the ground the more she was able to rescue and re-fashion. Arranging a circle of stones into an open stove, she lit a fire within it. The cast-iron cauldron on her father's work-bench was missing a leg but its belly was sound. Using water from the well-spring and some of the root crops, at least she'd have some nourishing soup... though a pinch or two of salt wouldn't go amiss. She remembered Pa's cache of home-baked biscuits, and soon found them tucked behind the tea cannister. That was next to the Primus as usual, the small pan at the ready. And, old as it was, the cow could still supply a drop of milk. Meagre fair to be sure, but still, she wouldn't starve.

Absorbed in her searching, she sensed a rustle of movement. Was something following her, stalking her? A farm hand seeking work? She froze. The sound stopped. She moved on, and there it was again. It didn't sound like the trot of a dog. Too timid for a bear, heaven forbid, though she'd only heard about those in stories. A goose perhaps? But whenever she glanced around, however suddenly, it was only the air she could see. Neither flea nor fowl nor any living thing. And yet, as she continued her inspection of the rutabagas, there it was. That rustling, that sound.

She began to carry a stick with her, whether for comfort or protection she couldn't tell you. But she chose a length of wood and stripped it clean of twigs. Her father had a tool store in the shed, and she'd helped him many times to smooth the splinters from a newly turned chair leg. First the coarsest sandpaper, careful not to scrape the skin of her thumb. Then a sheet of medium, which did most of the work. And finally, the smoothest for a finish to stroke like a talisman. She kept the walking staff propped just outside the door, ready and steady whatever the weather.

In her quest, Lottie had fattened enough courage to dare stray from the path. She kept the silo in sight, searching, ever searching. She was bent low, half hidden by tall grasses, when a cry startled her. "Ho, Little Missy!" It was Deet Filey, Butcher Bertie's boy. As she stood, he was right in front of her. "Long way from home, ain'cha?" he said.

"Listen," she commanded. "Did you hear that? That honk-honk?"

They both looked around, turning in a circle. At first Deet thought she was joking, playing a game. But she repeated, "That goosey noise. Didn't you hear it?" She swished her walking stick from side to side, hitting out at the grass. As though the stick had some effect on the weather, the grasses billowed out in the wind. Puffs of grey clouds hurried across the sky, eager to keep a celestial appointment.

"I never heard nowt nor nothing. What are you on about?" Deet had never spoken more than a greeting to her before. Was she off her chump? he wondered.

"Have you seen them?"

"Who?" She was scaring him. He'd never seen a child so fixed on anything.

"Ma and Pa. They're gone. And the house. Gone."

"Now, now, Little Missy..."

"Lottie!" she insisted. "My name is Lottie. I'm not a child."

"No, no... neither you are." In truth, he wasn't that much older.

She double-backed to the path, grabbing his arm. He let her pull him along. Well, there was no stopping her, really. As they approached the silo, Deet could see the cow shed, but Lottie was right. The house had vanished. She let go of his arm. "See," she pointed toward the empty space and began to run. "Come on if you're coming." Breathing heavily, he caught up with her just as the needles of rain drove them into the shed.

They both blinked at the change from daylight. Deet lifted the blanket from the cow stall to rub Lottie dry. In turn, she took on the task of making tea. They shared from the same enamelled metal mug, just as she had with Pa. Deet watched, quite helpless, as she began to sob.

"Where are they?" she implored him. "What's happened?" Her words blurred with tears.

"Where was they? Last time you seen 'em?" [The question his mother always asked if he'd lost something. Socks. Slingshot.]

Lottie described the last image she kept of her parents. Pa helping to tie the string around her mother's fingers. Of the homely smell of baking. And the two of them, united in a hug. Deet was as puzzled as the girl. "Well here's a bobble and no mistake." He examined the sky, predicted clear weather approaching. "Do you think you could walk a ways with me? Back to town?" She shrugged. She had no concept of what that might entail. "Anyroad, sure as eggs in the pulpit," said Deet, "you can't stay here."

They finished the tea and set off down the path. "Vamp on," he urged, striding ahead, then waited for her to catch him up. They lost sight of the shed, and suddenly Lottie stopped. "What about the cowie? Who'll feed her?"

Deet put his arm around her. He wanted to be her protector. "Never fret," he said. "Let's get you settled. Everything will work out." He gave her shoulder a fraternal squeeze and turned to face her. "Now, where are you hiding that smile, Little Missy?"

"Lottie," she protested. But she did smile at him.

*

They made it into town before dark. Lottie could barely keep her eyes open at the table, even when the butcher's wife served an enormous joint of roast lamb set about with crispy potatoes. The smell made her mouth water, and she'd never in her life seen so much meat on one plate. But she was exhausted, confused by the family's questions, and grateful when she was led upstairs to bed. It was clearly a girl's room: a colourful rag rug over the board floor, and a hand-embroidered counterpane brightened the single bed against the wall. Its pattern of rosebuds matched the window curtain.

The butcher's wife wished her good night. "She's that tired, poor lamb," she told her husband. "We'll get the story in the morning."

It was a large house, and the family rented lodgings to the workers, meals all in. There was plenty of room. The most experienced slaughtermen bunked in together, for the company. The three eldest Filey children had flown the nest a few years back... the two boys settled in separate county towns, one a bit closer to home, and their daughter braving the ocean to marry a sailor. Deet was their youngest, the only one left to help.

He shared one of the bedrooms with a farm hand called Jethro about his own age. Deet had learned about the inventor of the seed drill at school, and tagged him Tully. In turn he acquired the nickname Deet the Meat... sometimes extended to a rude rhyme, chanted straight-faced with mischief: you can't beat Deet the Meat! Lads with a careless, insatiable appetite for daring and derring-do. Verbal pissing contests: what would you do if...

But it had been a while since there was an actual girl in the house. They'd all have to mind their Ps and Qs.

It didn't take long before every family and shopkeeper in town learned the tale of Little Missy. Deet was right to assume they'd all club together to offer her food and board. Payment? Not to fret, she'd see them right when she could. Being best known to her parents, it fell to the Meat Master and his wife to provide the most of communal care.

They all sat round the table for breakfast, a generous array for the family and all the lodgers. Lottie tried to answer their questions, but there was so much she just didn't know. Then the butcher's wife remarked idly, "I'll wager that storm did some damage." Lottie looked blank. "You know, just a wee while ago."

"No," said Lottie, her mouth full of sausage. "There was no storm at the farm." She paused, trying to think back. "I did hear thunder over the hills, but the rain only fell yesterday." She gestured across the table with her tea cup. "Deet, you saw it."

Butcher Bertie screwed up his face in thought, his bushy brows pushed together like an enraged terrier. "Aha!" he said, and banged his flat palm on the table, scaring the youngest farm lad off his seat. "That's it!" he scanned their faces with a smile as triumphant as if he'd solved the mystery of Jack the Ripper. The rest looked puzzled.

"Right enough, Little Missy, not a storm at all." He paused for effect, such a natural performer. "A dust funny! Whirly thing, come out of the sky without warning, like a flock of geese diving on the grain. A dust funny! Yep, that's the fellah!" He tore off a lump of bread and wiped it round his plate to sop up the gravy. "Rare enough, but I mind a powerful one when I were a lad. Next parish but one. Quick as that." He snapped his fingers. "Everything gone." He named the place and the older men nodded. "Yessiree," he added. "Picked up the miller's grind-stone, a nest of rats, and the vicar's missus. Dumped them all somewheres else. Just like that." He snapped his fingers again.

"Beg pardon, Mister," asked Lottie. "Does that mean my parents might be dumped somewheres else as well?"

He looked to his wife, the small shake of her head advising him to move away from such speculation. They didn't always discuss everything, but assumptions helped glue them together. He couldn't recall a time they weren't together. He'd always been her Bertie, her dear heart, and she was his sweetmeat, Janet, the candle of his love.

It took the best of two years before Lottie could fully accept Bert Filey as her replacement father, and Missus Meat as her mother. "Might as well call me Auntie," she said, and Lottie did. She'd never had any siblings though, and her feelings for Deet were far from fraternal. Of course, she never forgot her parents, nor for a moment believed they wouldn't be found. Someday. For, as the saying goes, we live in hope that live at all.

The family grew to depend on her help wherever she could. Mistress of any task set to her, what she didn't already know she was canny enough to ask, and proved to be a quick learner. The law of the land decreed she'd have to attend school, but around these parts the law was flexible as a ferret. Her new family obligations required her to work with the butcher's wife, making classes compulsory only three times a week, and never on market days. She soon learned the cost of every cut from snout to tail, and could guess at the weight with an eye as keen as Butcher Bertie's.

"I don't know what we'll do when she ups and goes," Janet confided. She snuggled against her husband's wide chest, and he tightened his arm to contain her.

"It may not come to that," he said. He turned to blow out the bedside candle. "Our Deet seems keen."

*

Janet missed having her own daughter near, and was always on hand to help Lottie through the confusions of her early teen-aged years. Spots on her forehead, monthly tummy cramps, and – rare though they were – a sudden and irrational outburst. Between folklore and book learning, Lottie learned to trust this kind woman. She never complained at having to work for her lodgings; she was well used to that. Though not as handy at baking as her own mother, there were plenty of kitchen treats, even a few pamperings. Lottie blushed with pride when Auntie Janet hugged her, not quite a maternal coll, but genuine and uncomplicated. "I thank my lucky stars," she said, "the day you came to us." When she let go, Lottie could see a tear or two slide down her cheek.

One day she was scrubbing the stone walls of the outhouse. She'd pinned a posy of musk roses to her chemise to counter the smell, and was humming to divert herself from the task. Suddenly she felt rather than heard the door move. Two arms grabbed her from behind and turned her around. Tully the farmhand was trying to kiss her. His breath reeked of stale tobacco. She kicked out, but he held her fast. Then, just as he moved his face even closer, she saw him being yanked away. It was Deet, riding to the rescue. He landed Tully a sharp blinker that tinted the eye black and blue for weeks. They all staggered out into the sunshine, bent over their knees, breathing their recovery. Lottie ran to the house. She didn't look back to see the scuffle take a second turn. Both lads hit out with windmill arms before Deet landed a blow to the bellows and stalked off through the barley.

"Who needs ya, anyroad?" Tully crawled through the mud. "Better croak than stop here!"

The butcher's wife neither mocked nor doubted. She soothed the girl with a cool glass of sweetened lemon water, and dried her tears with a corner of her apron. The following day, none of the field hands was surprised when a new lad turned up in Tully's place.

She would never exactly blossom into beauty, but Lottie's happy nature brought smiles to all who met her. Although once, when she was helping at the market stall, a village woman approached. "Why, you must be Little Missy," she exclaimed. "You're the spit of your Ma."

"Do you know where she's at?" Lottie could hardly contain herself. The woman grew silent. Hasn't the child been told the truth? she wondered. It shouldn't be up to me to cite a death notice. She took the coward's way out. "Beg pardon, I've mistook you for another," she said and turned away.

"Who was that?" asked Janet.

Lottie shrugged. "I want to go back home... to the farm," she said. Neither argument nor delay would dissuade her, and off she went before the dawn.

She had no idea which road to follow, settling her trust on a skein of geese flying overhead. After a while she heard a rustling behind her. It was Deet. Loyal Deet. Not the ghost goose. He caught up and turned her off the path into an adjacent field. "Come on, follow me."

They walked for some hours, no space for idle chatter. Using markers of outcrop and stream, he led her through a thick copse into an unploughed field. Far off to its edge, they could make out the shapes of the stone silo and the shed. Lottie stopped, and Deet stood beside her, unclear what she wanted or how to help. Still she didn't move. "There it is," he said.

"Have you been inside, since... you know?" Without waiting for his answer, she ran all the way, and he trailed behind. Apart from the dust and cobwebs, everything was as she remembered. He lingered in the doorway, and she smiled up at him, her excitement infectious. "We could build it again, couldn't we? The house? Start here in the shed, look... strip out all this, fit some windows, a big front room, lots of light, and..."

But before she could say another word he bent down and kissed her on the mouth. She flung her arms around him. She'd been hoping that's what he would do, and she took it as an understanding, a wordless promise, a kind of engagement. "Will you help?" He nodded and kissed the tip of her sharp nose. But she pulled away and ran out into the yard. "Did you hear that?"

He followed. "That goosey sound? Honk! You must have... clear as clear!" Oh, no, he thought, not that again. He did the only thing he could to bring back her smile. He carried her into the cow stall and laid her down on the blanket atop the straw. The damp hadn't quite claimed it, and any biting chats had long since scurried away. She looked at his face as he guided her hand over his cheek and down his neck. Not quick and urgent like the bull. Slow and careful, trusting with a tinge of fear. They pulled clothes up and pushed them down. He watched her look of affection overcome her anxieties, about him and the ghost goose.

"Pa," Deet implored his father. "I been thinking."

"New experience, was it, son?" He carried a stack of plates to his wife at the sink. He winked at her.

"Don't tease him, love," she said, but even she couldn't suppress a chortle.

"No," Deet protested. "I meant..."

"I know that look. Only one thing to say to that look. What's it going to cost me?" He settled into the armchair to load his pipe for a smoke before bedtime.

"No, listen, Pa." Deet was collecting a pail of supper scraps for Sadie the yard sow and paused at the kitchen door. "They're bringing those new-fangled agricultural machines to the show. Thought we might take a look, is all."

"You're a chip off the block, young Deet, and no mistake. Happen we will." He blew out a puff of blue-grey smoke. "Been thinking the same thing myself."

Lottie had been drying the plates draining beside the sink and listening avidly. "I want to come with you." She wasn't asking permission.

Once Deet had declared his intentions toward Lottie, the butcher and his wife did what they could to prepare them for life as a couple. Rebuilding Lottie's farmhouse, restoring her land into a working unit, attracted volunteer helpers from miles around, many recruited from the shop's customers.

Over the years and long before she was born, Lottie's parents made a lasting impression on traders whether buying or selling. Their own memories of her mother's kindness and her father's ready humour assured a steady team every day to help with the construction work. No need for blueprints or fancy-pants architects, dwellings for centuries relied on the ancient physics of dry-stone walling and keystones. Every farmer had the basics passed down.

Meanwhile, Deet settled Lottie into his room, giving her Tully's bed. And should either tiptoe over for some spooning, clipsing, and colling beside the other, no one would chastise or trouble them whatever time of night.

The new lad was placed in the single room, rosebud curtains notwithstanding. Keeping Lottie in the family wasn't entirely a selfless act. Her inherited land ensured the expansion of the Fileys' mixed herds and offered every remedy to turn the stony arable into a bounty. Butcher Bertie had always played the long game.

Time was measured by progress on the new house. With such dedicated help it wouldn't be much longer before Lottie could move in. Then it would be for Deet to decide whether he'd follow on. She couldn't visit every day, but at least once a week she helped prepare the shire horses for a trip to the farm. She'd stopped speaking her hopes out loud, but Deet could tell she was ever on the look-out for some trace of her parents. And whenever she turned her head all of a sudden, he knew she'd caught the sound of the goose. Or thought she had.

Came the day - when the house was nearing completion – the Meat Master locked up shop and slipped harness, reins and leather traces around the dray horses. The whole family and all the lodgers climbed into freshly washed duds, abandoning all work and chores to meet up with friends and neighbours at the Candlemas County Show. Janet called Lottie upstairs; she fetched out a skirt of striped linsey-woolsey with a black grosgrain band around the hem. It had been left behind by her daughter, and although not a perfect fit, a few pins here and there left Lottie feeling like a picture in the Country journal. In place of her tight work cap, there was even a bonnet of woven straw, and sewn on with meadow poppies.

As she came back downstairs, Deet whistled through his teeth. "Don't you look grand, Little Missy."

He helped his mother to ladle lemon barley water into a couple of stoneware bottles and hung them with twine from his belt loops. Meanwhile, she prepared a picnic basket stuffed with savoury goodies, sugared cobnuts and other sweetmeats. Lottie took it on herself to bake a pair of apple cakes. Her mother's legacy.

So many attractions! Everyone had saved their pennies in anticipation of temptation. They tramped through fields and entered tents of livestock being readied for auction later in the day. The women lagged behind the others because Lottie had never before seen a show, and wanted to know what everything was. Breeds of cattle, farm gadgets and gee-gaws. Inside one of the tents, she paused at a pen of tiny piglets, squeaking for their mother, treading through a shallow pan of water. "Well, ain't they cute as a bug's ear!" And Lottie replied, "I'll have some when the time comes. Treat 'em proper." The butcher's wife was more mindful of consequences. "Leastways till they're up for rashers," she said as kindly as she could.

They caught up with the men, standing in a circle in front of the ice tent. Inside was a trestle table loaded with frozen blocks hacked from the Norwegian fjords, and delivered by canal barge onto sturdy drays. Casks of ale nestled between the ice slabs; customers paid a penny piece to hold their mugs under the spigot, filling them to the brim. The talk was of the new agricultural machine, pros and cons.

"Happen we can ask Mr Albone," said one man. "I'm of the same mind," said the Meat Master. "That's him holding the field trial, and he's the inventor. If he don't know, no one will!" Mugs clinked in agreement, then another man said, "Anyroad up, who's for the pony show?" Several of them peeled away to the riding paddock.

Deet said, "Come on, Pa, I want you to see those Belties down from Scotland... see if we put 'em to our Friesians, you reckon we could build a herd for myself and Lottie?" Lottie lowered her head as Janet gave her shoulder a squeeze. They both recognised Deet's question was in fact a marriage proposal. Lottie lifted her smiling face toward him. "Well," said his mother, "it ain't likely she's going to give him the mitten. Are you, dear heart? You won't refuse him, will you?"

The women found a grassy space free from mud and smoothed out two wide picnic blankets. The men followed their noses to the feast. It had been a morning of friendship and good cheer. Many a laugh shared and some tokens of affection pledged, though whether those might last through the night was hardly cause for a bookmaker's odds.

Lottie sat with her legs tucked under next to the butcher. She was peeling a hard-boiled egg; he was in conversation with some farm hands, earnest and confused. They relayed disturbing news from one of the auction tellers. "His son's signed up for the regiment. You'll know him, Mister, young Samuel."

"I mind him all right," the Meat Master puffed on his pipe. "Little scamp used to nick the pasties set out to cool!"

"Anyroad up, the talk's all of war. But behind closed doors, hush like." This was serious stuff; all three had lost uncles and granddads fighting for king and country in foreign jungles and across the Hindu Kush.

"Seems we're getting too big for our britches. Can't patrol the whole world forever."

"Right enough. They put their mark on the papers down London way, and it's our boys do the bleeding."

"King don't give a damn for the likes of us."

The Meat Master listened; he'd known these men for years, whether soused or sober. They'd always shared strong opinions about the state of the world, but he wondered how close they were getting to treason. "You lads ain't thinking of playing at cannons, are ya?"

"Take orders from some minted toff general, sucking on a dream stick and sticking his prick in the pick of the doxxies? Not bloody likely!"

"Nah!" another man agreed. "I'm keener on that harvest invention. Can do everything bar brew the tea, they say!" They rose to go. "See you there."

The butcher waved his pipe toward them in farewell. Lottie gathered the bits of egg shell and tidied them back into the basket. “What do you reckon, Little Missy? Think there’ll be a war soon?”

She really couldn’t calculate the import of his question, but she wanted a hopeful future. “Not before I move into my new farmhouse.” She brushed one palm against the other, a telling gesture.

After the field trial it didn’t take much prodding from Deet to convince his father to order the Ivel Agricultural Motor and clasp spit-hands with its inventor, promoter, and entrepreneur Dan Albone. They agreed a delivery date. “I’ll have yer warranty prepared, sir. Drive it to the farmhouse, I assume?”

The Meat Master nodded and licked the point of his pencil. He drew a rough but accurate map and handed it over, well chuffed at the prospect of setting the pace for the future. Albone ruffled Deet’s hair. “And will this young chap be the prime mover?”

Before he could reply, Lottie interrupted; she’d been following the transaction. “We’ll share the work, sir,” she said. “But I would also like something a bit more nimble to keep eyes on the darker corners.”

Albone exchanged glances of quiet amusement with Deet and his father. To Lottie he said, “You are clearly a clever girl. May I have the pleasure of learning your name?”

“I am Lottie.”

“And you may call me Dan,” he said holding out his hand to shake. As she did he continued, “Have you been following the tale of the Safety Cycle, Lottie?” She shook her head. “Won prizes all over the shop. Superannuated now, sad to say. It was my passion before field harvests took my fancy.” He patted the Machine on its rear wheel. “Of course, this little beauty itself took Gold at the Waverton Ploughing Match.” Lottie wasn’t sure what she was meant to say. “How would it be were I to include one of my cycles along with the Ivel? Gratis, of course. Would that do?”

No one was sure where Lottie had found such confidence. “That would do just fine, Dan, sir” she said.

He lifted the watch from its silvered fob chain across his suit vest. "Now, you'll all have to give me leave, I'm afraid. I'm due a delegation up from London."

*

She had just turned fifteen when Lottie could move into her new house. Old Lady-Day in April, the celebration marking a new start for the field hands contracted at Candlemas, and the first public day of her marriage to Deet. They chose the rural manner, no need for the solemn rites and gestures of church folk. Lottie remembered her father's sneer of clerical dismissal: "These vicars and bishops, clad in silks and golden thread, they shit in the privy same as us!"

She wove a circlet of green willow as a crown and Deet borrowed a smart bowler derby hat. Lottie giggled when she knuckled the stiff felt crown to hear the solid thwack. "Like knocking on a loaf to hear if it's baked," she said.

Deet winked at her. "I can knock on your loaf tonight, if you'll have me."

All the neighbours, stockmen and farm hands gathered under an ad hoc bower to witness the couple's joining of hands. The rings they placed on each other's fingers were fashioned from twisted grass. Snug fits, and ceremony enough. The guests sang and danced in the sunshine to seal the union.

Let those who will be proud and chill
For me, from June to June,
My Dolly's words are sweet as curds,
Her laugh is like a tune.
With a hey, Dolly! ho, Dolly!
Dolly shall be mine,
Before the spray is white with May,
Or blooms the eglantine.

And, adding even greater merriment, some even sang Hey Lottie, ho Lottie, Lottie shall be mine...

Those who could had donated furniture fit for every room. Deet and Lottie didn't have to purchase a thing. Auntie Janet had spent months knitting an over-blanket for the double-size bed. And, as a wedding surprise, the Meat Master had delivered the shiny new Agricultural Motor to the adjacent field, all tied up with a giant bow, the bicycle strapped to the side.

The couple decided to split the week, Deet spending three or four nights together, the rest with his parents to help with Pa's herd and run the market stall. It was left to Lottie to take charge of the farm on her own. Whenever she could spare the time, she steered her new cycle through the furrows of the field, searching, always searching.

Deet happened to be with her when a jaunty caravan appeared over the hill along the path. It was spruce in bold colours of red and blue and green, and pulled by a doe-eyed mule yoked to a small Fell Pony. The harness was studded with bells, which were also stuck around the bow-top cabin. Their jingling brought a jolly air, and as the vehicle grew near, Deet and Lottie heard the bounce of a fiddle. The tune landed smack at their feet, near impossible to resist, jigging into their bones. The musician was a young lad of seven or eight, but already expert on his three-stringed instrument. He stopped playing as the caravan drew up near the farmhouse.

The man driving the team dropped the reins and removed his pipe by its painted bowl. He adjusted the battered fedora back from his brow. "How do." He gestured to the boy, "That's Timbo, my son. If you like his tune he'll be happy with copper or what you can spare." A baby crawled out from the wagon, snatched up by a comfortable armchair of a woman; you just wanted to curl up in her lap. When she grinned at Deet and Lottie, they noticed one of her front teeth was missing. Her hair was loosely wrapped in a fringed scarf patterned with flowers of gold. On closer inspection she, too, was younger than expected, though certainly older than Lottie.

"Never mind all that, Patta," she rocked the baby against her enormous bosom. "Never mind him," she said to Lottie, "but some well water would go down a treat if you might spare some, Missus."

Lottie had never been called Missus. She turned around to make sure her mother wasn't stood behind. Then she recovered. "Of course. Water. There's the spring just there. Help yourselves."

Deet took his cue from Lottie to be helpful to the strangers. He approached the older man. "Let 'em off the harness if you like. Got some windfalls in the larder."

"Much obliged." He offered out his pipe. Not wanting to give offense by refusing, Deet pretended to take a puff before passing it back. Patta refrained from remarking at the closed-mouth cough Deet tried to repress.

Lottie went inside to fetch a few apples for the animals and one of her fresh-baked apple cakes, cooling on the kitchen table. When she came back she heard Deet ask, "Whereabouts you folks from?"

"Just over for the Appleby Horse Fair. Grand do, so it was. Caravans and vardoes far as the eye could see." Deet recognised the Gallic lilt of his accent; some of his father's seasonal farm hands spoke like that. The woman approached again, baby tucked under her arm. She took the cake from Lottie.

"There's kindness, Missus," she said. "Patta, tell 'em what we heard at the Fair."

It was the same news of imminent war that fuelled the rumours at the County Show. "You wanna watch out, fellah, till they feel yer collar for the army."

"Oh, no," Lottie protested. "He's needed here. Exemption." She'd recently learned that word and was proud to show it off.

The man chuckled. "Sounds like a medical condition, 'emption.' You'll need some embrocation."

Deet laughed, too, and so did Lottie, though she didn't really get the intent. Young Timbo returned from the well spring. He spoke with a light lisp. "Want me to round up the team, Pa?"

"There's no hurry," said Deet kindly. "You can park up here for the night if you like. Lottie?" She nodded agreement.

Timbo tugged at her skirt. "What's that honking, Missus?"

"What did you say?"

"I hear honk-honk, but don't see any goosies."

Deet was quick and caught her in his arms as she fainted against him.

*

For the Meat Master, keeping his workers from the regiment took too much of his attention. Nor was he able to prevent a couple of lads from trading their scythes for Brown Bess, as they called their new muskets. For his wife, trying not to bombard Lottie about grandchildren took much of her restraint. As for the happy couple, persistent horizontal frolics had so far failed to produce the patter of tiny toes, but they sure were having fun trying. Practice makes perfect, so they say.

After a couple of seasons building their herd of cross breeds, the pick of the litter of yard pigs, and enough steady layers to keep them well supplied with eggs, Lottie and Deet concentrated on enriching their soil for better harvests. They shared the Ivel machine with Bert, though it remained at their farm, tucked under a protective cloth at night. Chugging down the path at five miles an hour to Deet's family convinced Lottie she was a proper farmer.

The butcher regretted that Jake, his middle boy lived that bit too far over the hills for regular visits. Normally a forgiving man who walked on stony paths as easily as grass, he blamed the daughter-in-law for keeping him away. He could never remember her name... some dull Ruby or Lil he'd met at a county show where she'd found a day's work away from the summer fug of the town.

Both were sixteen, both the worse for the demon ale, she tossing her curls in his direction and he getting well and truly ensnared. Farm life would never tempt her. As for Jake, put the back end of a heifer next to his wife's and there was no doubting which orifice he'd always choose. Perhaps he was hen-pecked, perhaps not, but safe to say she led him by the nose-ring till his haunches quivered.

Parents are not meant to have favourites, but when Bert Filey examined his heart, Jake had held a special place from his birth. It wasn't for him to ask point blank if his wife felt the same. There were times, of course there were, when life turned against them, when he was powerless to protect her. Then he staved off the guilt with sheer toil, filling every working hour to improve their expanding empire. Yes, those bushy brows might give you a fright if you didn't know Butcher Bertie, but beneath the skin and sinew lurked the softness of a poet, though never so daft.

They'd already buried a baby boy who died at ten months with 'the fever,' as it was known, no actual doctor's diagnosis. [Far too dear, even if one might be summoned.] To stop his Janet's tears, he'd marked a tiny grave at the lush end of the field, under a rowan. Just the previous year she'd miscarried; neither of them could bond to clotted blood on the sheet, but he soothed her ague with strong tea and brandy. When baby Jake came along, he defied the midwife, insisting on being there to mop his wife's brow and count their blessings.

None of the Fileys had ever had much truck with church worship, preferring to mine family treasures over icons and Bible blabbings. From the milk of his own mother's breast, the Meat Master drank in the defiant resistance of his kin to any kind of authority. He couldn't recall how he learned the oaths of his Saxon ancestors, but even today, should he catch his thumb under the hammer, he'd shout "By the beard of Woden!"

From the first time she heard it, - when she was still known as Little Missy - Lottie fell in love with the phrase and repeated it, however inappropriately, to the amusement of the family. Deet, who had previously been embarrassed by his father [if the truth be told], eagerly followed Lottie's lead, and it became their own shared short-hand should a lamb go astray or a loaf fail to rise.

Every few months Bert Junior carted Elsie and the children home for Sunday lunch, joining Lottie and Deet and the resident slaughtermen. A jolly diversion from routine. Janet roasted a shoulder of lamb or rib of beef, plenty for everyone, as they all budged up to fit around the table. When they'd had their fill, the little ones toddled toward Aunt Lottie and Uncle Deet, the adults too busy dissecting the news of the day. The boy held out his arms for Deet to pretend to throw him away up to the ceiling, and Lottie knew the infant's coos and gurgles were an invitation to tickle her tummy. When Elsie caught her eye she held her arms close as though rocking a baby and pointed at her. But Lottie just laughed; she had enough of nods and winks, thank you very much.

While the war raged on, troop numbers kept declining. Reluctantly, the government sought advice to promote that old ploy patriotism to make up the numbers. Throughout the land notices announced the draft was coming... to a sign-up station near you! Enlist to do your bit! Everyone wanted to believe the auction ring wisdom: "It will all be over by Christmas."

Wary as they were, folk wondered whether they could hear the enemy crashing into their barns and byres, though it was less clear who the enemy actually was. Both Deet and his father rested uneasily, knowing their military exemption as food producers might be revoked at any time. Then they learned, too late, that Bert Junior and Jake had already joined up, serving together in the same regiment, news received with a combination of sadness and impotence.

The lads weren't allowed to say exactly where they were, but it was away from England, across the Channel. Before long the brothers wrote jointly to their parents, requesting supplies and sweetmeats which were shipped out to them without delay from the office in the High Road. All deliveries commandeered and monitored by the army. Gotta keep an eye out for contraband.

"Off they trot without so much as a by-your-leave," muttered their father, "and it's muggins here has to jump to it!" But he was glad to spoil them what with reports of war's unwelcome turns.

Early on in the conflict, such requests were easily met by local lads who'd been co-opted to help. They knew exactly whom the parcels were for... childhood mates and school friends. But when they too had been tempted by the king's shilling, the forces replaced them with low-ranking men, rejected from the front lines, strangers far from home, beholden to no one. Then the soldiers' hopes for treats often remained on the shelf, hand-written advice across the order citing "packet undeliverable," or "goods damaged in transit." And some crafty dodger upped his rations while the butcher's lads learned to choke down greying lumps barely recognisable as meat.

Some months later came word in a telegram, addressed to Mr Albert Filey. He remembered the buff-yellow paper even more than the message. Funny that. "It is my painful duty to inform you that Private Second Class Albert Filey Junior has been reported missing in action, as of this day inst. Lord Kitchener expresses his sympathy in the absence of further details." The curt message was signed 'Secretary War Office.' No name. The butcher bumped down onto one of the kitchen chairs, a dead weight. His wife stood over him, cupping his head against her apron. She was too stunned to cry.

The following week, Elsie turned up with the kiddies; she'd walked a fair bit of the way, and didn't know where else to go. She'd also received a telegram, though the delivery was a bafflement. Like the butcher's, it was also addressed to Mr Albert Filey. Exactly the same message. A husband, a son. All the same to Lord Kitchener. Then the tears flowed all right. Enough for an ocean. Deet thought they'd drown in it.

He knew there really wasn't room here with his parents; he and Lottie offered Elsie lodgings with them. Awaiting 'further details.' It wasn't ideal given the circumstances, but without Bert Junior's wages, she'd already been evicted from their rented rooms. The Fileys couldn't allow her to be sent to the workhouse, up to her shoulders in laundry suds, daily rations of hardened bread and mouldy cheese, fenced off from the children. Should Bertie ever return someday, whatever would he say to that?!

"Be nice to have some female company for a change," Lottie smiled. The baby, now a confident explorer, hid under her skirt. She plucked her out. "Though we may need to keep this one under a barrel!" And even Elsie had to chuckle through her misery.

Sometime later, Jake wrote his parents in pencil, admitting his wife had left him. 'Guess you was right, Pa.' But the message in his uneven hand didn't convey much else; it was redacted with heavy crossings-out. Even with all the town gossip and cattle market whispers, no one knew where he was fighting. And, if they did, they weren't telling. The butcher folded the short note, tucked it away in his work vest pocket, and kept it with him always. Always.

As the months turned to memories, the family's hopes for Bert Junior were fast fading. Elsie, glad at first of Lottie's friendship, began to feel she was an intrusion, an alien thing wholly composed of imminent grief. And despite her best self, she sensed her children sought the comfort of Aunt Lottie and Uncle Deet over her own maternal care. A baseless fear, but there it was. When she got word her widowed mother had been confined to her bed, Elsie decided to travel over the hills to care for her. No fuss, no forwarding address, no farewells. Who could tell when she might return?

By now reconciled to their own childless marriage, both Deet and Lottie remarked how quiet the house was without Bert's brood. They were stating facts, not hopes to the contrary.

War had its own plans. Despite America's insistence to remain neutral, everyone knew the Yanks had sailed over, goaded by profit-hungry moguls into testing out armaments on the battle field. After several failed inciting incidents, in May 1917, the London Times ran a double-column spread recounting the sinking of the Lusitania out of Liverpool, with a map pin-pointing where the enemy had struck. The filthy Hun! Even the ultra-cautious US Congress blazed with righteous fury and approved military vengeance.

"Over there, over there," they sang in the streets. "Send the word, send the word over there, That the Yanks are coming..."

Into Europe they trooped, spreading across the map like ink blots. They were assigned temporary billets, and the locals had to like it or lump it. Some villages welcomed their good-humoured boasting and especially their generosity with smokes and chewing gum and Dixieland dance steps. For others, especially those who had already lost loved ones to foreign mud, it was too little, too late.

Another telegram. The butcher's wife was away with Deet at the market when a uniformed lad rode up to the shop on his regulation bicycle. The Meat Master didn't want to open the envelope and placed it under a suet tray, just the corner sticking out. But when his young apprentice brought him a mug of tea, freshly brewed, he slipped into the back room and read the news. No mistake this time. No loose ends or false hopes. Jake was dead. "A credit to his regiment," according to Lord Kitchener. As though he'd actually known him.

The telegram made it sound as though he'd been killed in battle, but neither Lord Kitchener - who couldn't have cared less - nor Albert Filey - who cared beyond caring - ever learned that in the dark shadows of his madness he'd contrived to hang himself. Jake, his precious boy, his little sausage. He looked around the room, the very room where he'd chased the little sausage under that very table, pretending he was a big hungry bear come to eat him for supper.

When the apprentice came to find him, he sat there still, the tea cold on the table.

*

They called it the war to end all wars, though it didn't, and not many believed it would. When the Armistice with Germany was signed by Supreme Allied Commander Marshal Foch, it wasn't only cheeky school-boys shouting 'Foch you,' into streets and midnight alleys. So-called victory barely made a difference to rural life. The demands of the land were relentless in war and peace. Though government devolved social welfare assistance to local urban charities, – 'Let the poor take care of themselves' - their agenda was different for farmers and food producers. The shameful strategy was to set them against rural labour, tithing harvests for wider distribution, rationing basic staples 'for the greater good.'

Towns were easy: planning maps and census documents, noted and filed away, safe in clean, familiar buildings. Decisions enacted behind office desks, sipping sugared tea. Milk or lemon, sir? Biscuit, sir? Civilised. But inhabitants of land beyond the beyond were a matter of guesswork. Never enough inspectors to muddy their boots through droughts and thunder storms, not to mention question marks over exact ownership. Benefit of the doubt was always awarded to toffs with proper paperwork, even though illiterate families had held their land from Saxon days. If it wasn't written down, their claim simply didn't exist.

Lottie and Deet fumed. No wonder the very notion of politics brought up their bile. They agreed: we can't tell the cowies to stop their milk nor the seeds to rest in the ground. But they both worried how the news of the older Filey boys had knocked the wind from his parents' bellows. Too many field hands on both farms had also perished, far, far away, marked only by the mud where they fell. Soon washed away. Gradually the couple picked up the business slack.

Butcher Bertie, unable any longer to ignore his painful joints, agreed with Janet that Deet should take over the shop. He altered the sign on the window: Filey & Son. Pride and sadness. When the pen-pushers down South gave word they'd done a deal for 400 Saunderson Tractors, Deet went half with his father to replace the old Ivel. Lottie wouldn't scrap it, though; it represented too much. Her independence and the days of the past.

She was driving it up and down the field when she spotted a man walking slow and steady along the path. She braked the machine and shaded her eyes against the autumn haze. Looked like the man had a dog with him. Something familiar. Couldn't be, could it? The man got closer. It was... it was Bert Junior! Lottie jumped off the machine and ran up to meet him. "Bertie!" she cried.

"Is that Lottie?" There was so much to tell, so much to ask that their words kept bumping into each other. Instead, they just stood for a moment of reflection. Lottie noticed the dog was very well behaved indeed, neither barking nor jumping up, just sitting at Bertie's side, held by its harness. And she suddenly understood the man was blind.

"May I pet him?" She stooped down, hand poised over the pale fur of the Labrador.

"She's a she. Venus, my faithful companion."

"Come into the house, Bertie. You're both very welcome."

"Just lead the way; Venus will follow you."

"Deet should be back soon." She was aware how formal she'd become, as though the loss of Bertie's sight imposed a new etiquette. "We have a tractor, now." What was the right thing to say? She was so excited to hear his tale, this man who'd come back from... where? From the 'missing.' From 'further details.' Out of respect for the Filey family, though, she suspected she'd best wait for Deet.

To plug the time, she filled a bowl with water for the dog, and made a pot of tea. "Do you take it black or with milk? Forgive me, I can't remember." She poured him a cup and placed his hand on a small bowl in front of him. "Here's the sugar lumps, Bertie, just help yourself. Spoon's just here, look... oh, no, sorry, sorry. I only meant..." He laughed to help bridge her awkwardness. "Would you care for a ginger biscuit?" Safer ground with biscuits!

"Well, this is nice," he said, as though he were a vicar on a visit. Lottie watched as he mastered the map of the tea things on the table. She patted the dog and held out her hand to let her get a sniff. Venus wagged her tail. "She likes you," Bertie said.

"Deet's usually on time. He'll be so pleased to see you."

"What was that noise I heard back along the path? Sounded like a goose. Venus barked at it. Didn't you, girl?" He crunched on his biscuit. "You keeping geese now, Lottie?"

The slowing crick-cracky putt-putt-putter of the tractor drowned out her attempt to reply, and then Deet stepped in, and the kitchen came alive with laughter and tears and caution and hurrah. "If this don't beat all!"

Finally some calm claimed them, and Bertie was able to tell his story. Their day workers had already packed up, so the evening became his arena. He spoke for hours, and they took it all in. No room for many questions, not even stopping during the supper Lottie prepared as he talked.

It was no surprise [they discovered] that the army couldn't confirm his whereabouts. With concussion and so many injuries, he'd only recently been able to piece the bits together himself. For all the gaps of memory, he did recall the early days of his induction, billeted with Jake, training to become defenders, killers. Not the actions of the farmer, neat and tidy, laced with respect and accepting dispatch as a link in the food chain. No, he was becoming a cold blooded killer whose enemy for the moment was invisible.

Then he and Jake drew separate assignments. Neither knew where; Bertie couldn't even remember saying good-bye. Deet and Lottie silently agreed to keep the news of Jake's death till afterward. They were both fascinated by Bertie's flashes of random images.

Sitting in the back of a lorry crowded with uniformed strangers. Full doughboy gear, tin helmet, bayonet, tightly-wound puttees wrapped around woollen socks under boots that were too big. Bumping up and down over rocks in the road. Sharing a smoke with the squaddie squashed in beside him. And finally arriving at the sprawl they called camp. Then back to the shadows of his mind, clouding out from A to B, from here to there, from sight to insight.

Over time unrecorded he discovered some truth. He learned to connect clues in the half-heard conversations of others, and that the power of the past could often be released by the shape of a surface, a certain wall pattern, or inhaling odours, whether sweet or foul.

Apparently, his unit had accidentally been led behind enemy lines by a jumped-up Captain, an arrogant bully who'd never learned to read a map. His paunch, pocked skin, and rheumy eyes earned him the nickname Bullfrog in the ranks; it was not uttered with affection. He'd already lost nearly half of his assigned command to bad decisions, but he pushed on regardless. Always blameless in the eyes of the powers-that-be, accepting his false reports.

Bertie pronounced his name as though it were venom: Lyttelton-Sloane. The man had such undisguised contempt for the lower ranks, and, drunk or sober, didn't always keep it to himself. He blamed them for being in this shit-hole... keeping him from Mummy and Father's county seat and his Chester Square rooms, so handy for his club, where a chap could bathe and boister and do what the deuce he pleased when he pleased, dammit.

"Weren't for you ruddy shower, I'd likely be Major by now. Even Colonel. Dammit!"

"Bullfrog's off on one," said the soldiers.

Some of the more audacious men had tried to reason with him, to no avail. He swigged from the brandy flask in his jacket pouch pocket. "This way, you turds, or I'll have you up for treason." At the Bullfrog's orders, the troops hid in a thicket, building several campfires, blatantly and carelessly advertising the bivouac.

As they nodded off, the trees seemed to come alive, tossing a box of D5 grenades into the embers. Only a handful survived. Lyttelton-Sloane writhed in agony, both legs blasted off. Not one soldier came to his aid. A bullet might have been a kindness, but no one felt that kind. The others, including Bertie, were captured, taken to a German infirmary, unable to speak the lingo.

Though they were treated within the rules of war, Bertie's cotton-wool brain failed to make any sense. Was he back in England? Why couldn't he see? Why couldn't he hear in his left ear? And most of all, why didn't he know who he was?

It was only after the Armistice with Germany that the Allied command swept up lone prisoners, arranging priority re-patriation back to Blighty for those with the best prospects for recovery. There Bertie was placed in a rehabilitation facility, spending a couple of years learning to cope without sight, trying desperately to remember his life before the war, and wondering, wondering, whether he ever had a family, parents, a wife and kiddies.

Neither Lottie nor Deet could do anything but listen, tightening the grip on their clasped hands when the tale dripped with particular horror.

At last Bertie paused, reached down and stroked the dog. "Then I met this young lady and she saved my life. Don't know what I'd do without her."

"So," asked Deet hesitantly, "you haven't been to see Ma and Pa? Elsie? The children?"

It took quite a while to synchronise the nation's medical records, which accounts for the wide-ranging disparity of between fifty and a hundred million estimated deaths from influenza over the course of the war. But though the epidemic finally called a halt to itself, folk succumbed to its symptoms for years. So much had been lost: no generation was unclaimed, and the empty shops along the High Roads of the county bore witness to the need for public rescue. They hadn't just fought against a human enemy, it had also been a war with microbes, and that was a war no one could ever win.

Janet had been tending her husband's decline, the pain in his hips now almost unbearable. But when Deet brought his brother back to the Filey farmhouse even Butcher Bertie hopped up to greet him with no small irony "Daze my eyes!" and their mother wept with the joy of it. All the Fileys had to adjust for the future. Of course, not every generation has to make room for the common destruction of family life rent by disease and the cruelty of war.

They had to negotiate the simple logistics; it was a bottom line calculation. Making ends meet had become a teave and a struggle. Was it sensible to maintain two working farms as well as the shop and abattoir? With Butcher Bertie unable to make much of a contribution, should they parcel out their time to avoid the expense of hiring in experienced field hands?

The loyal slaughtermen tried to get a bank loan so they could buy the abattoir, giving the Fileys some needed cash and assuring the place would be in good hands. But they might as well have begged a loan from Ebenezer Scrooge. They were forced to accept a paltry amount and sign on the dotted to pay outrageous interest rates. And a no default clause. Whatever that meant. After all, they weren't lawyers.

Bert might rant all he liked against the ways that "them down London way" had grabbed such control of their lives, but he wanted to put things right for the family. He'd always put them first with a natural understanding that his love and Janet's was unconditional. Each day they'd succumbed to the spiral of mortality, perhaps the most potent lesson of farm life. They accepted without question the gravity of the grave, the destination of us all, and Bert probably sooner than later.

For now, there was his son, more stranger than son. A damaged man trying to remember, trying to regard this place as home, trying to find a way to belong. And there was this dog. A beauty, right enough, no trouble at all; but for the Meat Master, dogs were for fields, bedding in sheds and steadings, and commanded by whistles away to the hills. Not for kitchens.

Truth to tell, the rural customs of the past were no help. As were so many, Bert Junior and Elsie were a common-law couple. Yes, they'd called each other husband and wife, though Bert still couldn't remember the ceremony or even Elsie's surname. Nor was the army able to trace her. They just didn't know where to begin. No name. No known address. And, if they'd admit it, neither the time nor the inclination to track a person of such little importance.

Lottie and Deet strained to think whether she'd given them any clue where she was headed, where her ailing mother lived. Unschooled, she'd never learned to read and write; as the saying goes, 'anything a woman needs to know is between her legs.' Words even if spoken blew away on the wind.

At last it was decided. Bertie and the dog would stop on Lottie's farm. She captained the changes, scaling down the herd and ploughing under the crops they couldn't use themselves. Back in town, Deet reorganised the workload for his parents: field, shop and weekly market. If ever the Fileys had looked forward to the comfort of slowing down, feet up and telling tales, it wasn't to be. Their days of toil left them depleted, body and mind. And one morning Bert awoke to find Janet lying dead beside him. Those who knew diagnosed the influenza they thought had vanished from the town.

The butcher was inconsolable. Janet, the candle of his love. He cried like a lost lamb, open-mouthed and bleating, all spittle and snot. Deet and Lottie held him through his pain, and clung to each other. Tears, a poultice for comfort, but words died in their mouths. As for blind Bertie, he'd come to accept that Janet and Bert were his parents, though he still struggled to understand what that signified. It was only by relating such loss to his Venus that he was able to join the others in their grief.

As relative outsiders, so to speak, the dog and Bertie walked Lottie's land, criss-cross and obeying the abandoned furrows. Up and down, day after day. When the spring blooms opened Bertie sniffed the air and said, "It's the nosegay from your wedding, Lottie."

"Fancy you remembering that," she said. Another day, when she slipped in the mud and had a job standing, she let forth with "Damn patches and buggery!"

Instead of Bertie's laughter she heard him sobbing. Back at the house, warm and safe, he tried to explain over a cup of tea. "So much mud. Wherever we went. It was vile. Mixed with blood and shit and decay. Make you retch."

Butcher Bertie never recovered from Janet's death. It wasn't even a year later that he followed her to the grave. Some said it was a stroke, others a broken heart. Yes, there was a double plot reserved for them near the parish church, despite their ecclesiastical infidelity. And it was Lottie and Deet who organised the burial; the local mason had been a customer and carved the simple headstone as a gift. "Albert & Janet Filey, together through life and beyond."

*

Now, once upon a time there was a farm, a run-down affair at the end of a rocky lane. Just there beyond that copse, see it? The hand-built silo and farmhouse, the rough-hewn shed. There's an old-fashioned agricultural motor, look, in the middle of that field. Funny old thing, not a tractor, sort of a car but not a car either.

Walking through the field was a woman, swaddled in a woollen jacket, fastened to the neck barring the autumn wind. Her dark hair was hidden under a close-fitting cap, tied under her chin, just a curl escaping along her brow. Yes, it was Lottie, supported by her sturdy walking stick. Just beside her were a man and his dog. Bertie and Venus. Watching them from the farmhouse doorway was another man. Deet.

They'd already covered quite a distance and approached the borders of the copse. They both stopped, listening intently.

"It's the goose," said Bertie.

Lottie hid her anxiety with a bit of bravado. "Better not let me catch him till I roast his gizzards in his own dripping!"

Suddenly Deet heard Venus barking. Relentless and carried far up the hillside. Lottie turned around and waved, beckoning him to join them. Cautiously she and Bertie approached the line of trees, looking up at their tangled branches that formed a kind of cage.

"I reckon something's caught up there," he said.

"Can you really see the goose, Bertie?"

"Don't be daft. In case you hadn't noticed, I'm blind!" he laughed. "But I can hear it, same as you. Same as Venus." The dog continued to bark.

Then, as Deet came up to them, they heard a slow, sharp crick-crack. The sound of old wood breaking from its pith. It all happened in a few seconds. As they dodged the fallen branch they looked up again, just in time to see a pair of skeletons, tightly entwined in an eternal embrace, fall down at their feet. Freed after all these years. Venus stopped barking and a fat, greylag goose waddled up. It opened its bright orange beak and filled the air with Honk-honk-honk!

Lottie knelt beside the bones of her parents. "That's Pa's neckband," she said. "And look at Ma's fingers." Sure enough, wound deep into the bone was the string reminding her to take out the cakes lest they burn. Gently, Deet pulled her up. She'd begun to cry, but said, "I'm so happy, Deet. I've found them. I've finally found them."

"Let's get back to the house, eh. Come along, Bertie, back home now."

But when they looked around for the goose, it was nowhere to be seen.

As they crossed the field, Bertie held tight to the dog's harness. He began to sing. It was an old nursery tune and soon Deet and Lottie joined in.

Goosey goosey gander,
Whither shall I wander?
Upstairs and downstairs
And in my lady's chamber.
There I met an old man
Who wouldn't say his prayers,
So I took him by his left leg
And threw him down the stairs.

*

The seasons came and went and built up into years. Loved ones and strangers, folk lived and died, for that is the way of it. But if you looked hard enough, you'd see Lottie, much older now, and still walking through her farm. Her beloved kin gone yet still there. No longer searching, her questions resolved. Out of sight, never out of mind.

The ghost goose wasn't always in attendance. Other folk to nibble, Lottie supposed. But when it appeared, fat and sassy, and, though it coughed the occasional honk! into the air with a throat full of feathers, she'd made it her friend. You might even say she'd grown to love it.

***

KWICKIE KAPTION 3

Although he had no formal academic training, many historians and scholars regard Leonardo di ser Piero da Vinci [1452-1519] as a "Universal Genius" or "Renaissance Man." He was a prodigious inventor, devising helicopters, military tanks, diving suits, even rudimentary robots, though none could be built at the time. It was the combination of science and art which is his lasting legacy, including drawing, painting, sculpture, architecture, science, music, mathematics, engineering, literature, anatomy, geology, astronomy, botany, paleontology, and cartography.

Perhaps he's best known for The Mona Lisa, consistently deemed the most popular portrait ever made.

Leonardo: Why are you smiling, Signora Ghirardini? No one told you to smile.

Mona Lisa: Just wait till that fart hits you, Leo.

CHAPTER FIVE – THE ROUND TABLE

Automat **1927** **Edward Hopper**

Born in 1882 in New York's affluent Rockland County, Hopper's life was driven by rebellion. Despite his comfy childhood and the usual choice of his class, his parents eventually supported his art studies. His long career and prolific output saw him reject and be rejected by more genteel, mainstream subjects and techniques. His proudest pieces are classed within the so-called Ashcan School, celebrating the sinister, more complex layers of American life.

Automat, painted in 1927, is a potent example of the way Hopper br oke new ground in his influence on surrealism - abstracting blocks of contrasting colour within a predominant darkness. Its roots hold fast in realism, yet closer regard raises many questions of logic. This is particularly true of the lighting, so that the woman depicted is totally accessible but transcends time and place. There's a clear path to the bold, colour-block works of Mark Rothko, Roy Lichtenstein, and especially American Ben Johnson's pop-art nudes.

The woman is known to be Hopper's lifelong comp anion, model, muse, and manager of his work, Josephine Nivinson, though she was older and more voluptuous. She also shared his social values.

Merely placing her in an automat in the rumoured run-up to the Great Depression, gave contemporary viewers clues to her lack of innocence. Too many later interpretations fail to give enough weight to the changing nature of class divisions in American society, implicit in the painting.

As for the concept of the automat itself, the transplantation from its mittel-Europa origins to the disheartened American east coast cities, notably Philadelphia and New York, provided the novel combination of the automatic delivery of food, appealing to the sassy sense of louche fun in the Jazz Age. But it also normalised the growing reliance on technology being exploited by the drivers of a military agenda which would explode into World War II... an agenda that would widen the gap between rich and poor which cannot be recovered.

I hope the characters in my story convey something of the era's inherent subversion, as well as its pretence.

THE ROUND TABLE

"So I seen youse here, sittin' on yer lonesome, and I sez to myself, this little lady must've missed the bus." The young man flicked his thumb over his shoulder in the direction of the station.
Fog blurred the lights in the street. It was some hours ago that autumnal darkness had descended like a theatrical curtain onto the Great White Way of Manhattan. Although the automat was open late, most of the diners had left, for home or other beckoning pleasures of the night.

Some tables were square, a few were round with marble tops. Easily cleaned. The young man stood facing the girl at the round table. She wore a yellow hat, a bottle-green coat, and an air of sadness, almost despair.

"So, am I right or am I not wrong?" The man didn't sit down. That would have been too forward, and besides the seat was already occupied by her handbag. He saw a fleeting smile wipe the melancholy from her face and offered his hand to shake.

"What's yer name, doll?" She didn't take his hand, nor look up from the brim of her cloche hat, but continued to grasp her coffee cup. The man noticed she still wore one black glove, but had unfastened her coat. The table was adjacent to the oval-column radiator which blasted out enough heat to warm the whole block.

"Whaddya, come in from Philly?" Still, the girl said nothing.

Undaunted, the man pressed her for some contact, some connection. "Let me be Frank," he said. After a slight pause, he added, "because that's my name. Frank."

That line usually got a laugh with the dames. He waited, noting she hadn't asked him to leave nor called for assistance from the waiter at the far end of the room. When he next spoke he took her part in a fantasy conversation, shifting to a treble tone.

"Howdja do, Frank. I'm..." He started guessing names for her. "I'm Maisie. No? Lizzie? I'm..."

"I'm waiting for someone," she interrupted. Then returned her fleeting glance back to the cup. From his vantage point he could see there were only the dregs left.

Her brief glimpse tagged him as a man not much older than herself, spiffy and eager to make a good impression. His collar was starched; he was clean-shaven, hair and nails trimmed, jacket buttoned over his shirt and woollen vest. She refused to be intimidated; she'd been raised in a family of three older brothers, and she guessed this fellow considered himself 'some pumpkins.'

Frank peered through the large window past the gloom, across to the bus station. "So, would that be waitin' for someone comin' in or someone comin' back? If ya don't mind me askin'."

She didn't reply, but Frank caught sight of the tear threatening to escape from her eye. "Hey, little lady, don't cry."

"I'm not," she sniffed. She looked up as he offered his handkerchief.

"It's clean," he said.

"Thank you. You're very kind."

She looked like she'd been stood up good and proper, poor kid, he thought. "How long ya been here?"

"I'm not sure," she said. She dabbed her eyes and tried to return the handkerchief.

"Keep it," he said, as though he had one in every pocket. She blew her nose as discreetly as she could manage in the circumstances.

"May I sit down?" She nodded, and he moved her bag onto the table. "Why doncha spill... give Uncle Frank the low down, eh? What's yer name for a start?"

She hesitated for a moment, then looked him full in the face. "Wilma," she said... and told him a tale of a small-town girl wanting to better herself in the big city. Not exactly original, it happened every day. Nothing about her story surprised Frank, but she looked so fragile, he could only listen.

"I met a man on the bus," she said. "He told me he'd show me around, point me in the right direction. Said he'd treat me to supper." She started to cry again, wiping her eyes, turning her face away. "I must look just awful!"

"Nah! Swanky as they make 'em. The cat's pajamas." He wasn't fibbing; she was a pip all right. A real 'classy chassis.'

She looked across the room where the waiter was writing something on his order pad. "I'm not sure how much longer I can stay here." Her voice was small, as though it were being held captive.

"Yeah," Frank agreed, "even the waiters gotta go home sometime. You gotta place to stay?"

She shook her head. "May I trouble you for the time; you've already been so kind."

He pushed up his shirt cuff, revealing a gold-plated watch face like the ones advertised in her favorite movie magazines. He held out his wrist to her across the table, and she brought it up to her face for a closer look.

Suddenly she was taken by a violent coughing fit and grabbed his arm tighter. She wiped her mouth with the handkerchief he'd given her, and popped it into her handbag. "Sorry," she said, breathing her recovery.

Frank felt fairly helpless. "You okay, doll?" he said, and signalled across to the waiter. He mimed drinking a glass of water, universally understood even by staff at the automat. When Wilma had taken a modest gulp and thanked him, Frank wanted to keep her talking. She really was some looker, all right, tears and all.

He said, "So what else did this jelly bean tell ya?"

"Well, he brings me in here, sits me at this table, never shuts up. He says, 'I'll take you to Paris, France. I'll take you to Ruby Foos.' What a corny line, eh? Straight off the cob!"

They shared a laugh. "Hey, I could take you to Ruby Foos. You like rice, doncha?"

Wilma shrugged.

"Yeah, well he sure sounds a wrong number all right." The silence between them didn't qualify as comfortable. Frank needed to proceed with caution. "So lemme guess, the wisenheimer promises you the moon then takes a powder. Am I right or am I not wrong?"

She sniffed back any further tears.

"I better not catch him down a dark alley. I'll boff him one he won't forget!"

"Oh, Frank... it's even worse than that. He lifted my suitcase. Everything I own!" She sipped at the water. "Can't even afford this dog soup let alone another cup of Joe."

"No problem, doll. The Java's on me. Wanna refill? Something to eat?" She shook her head. "Don't be shy. When's the last time you ate somethin'?"

Her answer got trapped in her throat; she suppressed another coughing fit. "Piece of that custard pie they got over there." She nodded her head toward a sign reading Pie Section, displaying the rows of little glass doors which opened automatically with the insertion of a nickel or two. "It was very nice."

"Yeah, but ya can't live on pie! Wait here, I'll getcha a sandwich." He nodded in the direction of the waiter as he balanced the small plate back to the table and set it in front of Wilma. He watched her restraint as she bit delicately into the crust. She fingered the crumbs from the corners of her mouth.

When she finally met his gaze he asked, "So, wot are ya... hoofer? Canary in a club?"

"You sure ask a lotta questions. Whaddya, writing a book?"

Frank didn't want to rouse her suspicions any further. "Nah... I was just tryin' to help, is all."

"Yeah," Wilma said, softening. "You're very kind."

"So, bein' serious... Whaddya goin' to do now? I mean tonight." She shrugged again, and looked across the street to the bus station. "Seems to me, ya got three options."

"How do you figure that?" she asked.

"One... you try and get a bus home... Some of 'em run all night. I know, I know, you ain't got no do-re-mi, but you drop a dime, call your folks, and they get the cash, and hand it over to the bus driver. All hotsy-totsy."

"Yeah, well, we ain't got a telephone," said Wilma, "let alone the money."

"Okay, so number two... which is also number three. I loan you somethin' to get you on your feet. I mean I ain't no Rockefeller but it's somethin' and you pay me back when you can." Wilma looked up sharply to see if he was being serious. Frank held out a rolled-up wad of dollar bills.

"I ain't hard to find. Only you gotta choose whether you sleep on a bench in the bus station, which is option two... or I walk you over to the YWCA. It ain't far, cross-town on Lex. Lexington. Avenue."

"Are you sure?" Wilma was almost speechless. He nodded, waving the cash at her. She took it and tucked it into her handbag. "I'll just go and powder my nose." To be polite, Frank stood when she did. "I'll be right back," she said as she descended the steps to the toilets. He waited for nearly an hour before he knew he'd been had. The scammer scammed!

*

"Wotta chump I am!" Frank confessed to his Jersey City pals a week later. "Tell youse what, though. This dame, smooth as smooth. A dip supreme, she took my watch off me, I never even felt it."

"Can't believe you gave her all your lettuce. Sounds like a couple a quarters would've done."

"You took the bait, hook, line, and sinker!"

They threw him a series of shadow-box punches. He brushed them aside. He was hoping they'd see how he tried to do the right thing. For all the good it did him.

"She played me for a patsy, all right!"

"Must've been some special doll to get one over on you, Frank."

"Oh yeah, she was grinchy, all right. A real Sheba."

"A real worker, ya mean... she got ya on the flimflam." They kept teasing him.

"Ah, yer father's mustache! Betcha any one of youse would've done the same."

"Yeah, yeah."

"I mean you wanna see them gams. All the ways up to her..."

"I think we get the picture, Frank!"

*

It had been raining for most of the day. Frank lit a cigarette for comfort, and sought shelter in the automat. Cuppa Java sure would hit the spot. He bought a nickel token from the cashier and collected a cup and saucer. He placed the cup under the spout in the shape of a dolphin, thumbed the token into the slot, and watched the dark brown liquid fill just the right amount. Still the best brew in town.

The large lunchtime crowds had long gone. Many tables were occupied - couples meeting up for a night at the pictures, lady friends comparing their department store indulgences, some lonely businessman. But there was some space nearer the door.

Still holding his coffee, Frank approached the small round table. Marble top. Easy to clean. The girl in the yellow cloche hat lifted her head. Her green coat with the coney collar was unbuttoned and her handbag was on the chair opposite. Neither Frank nor Wilma spoke. They just stared at each other.

***

CHAPTER SIX – THE PAINTED LADY

Woman in a Purple Coat 1937 Henri Matisse

Whenever a fiction film begins with the words 'Based on a true story,' something in me resists. How do you know, I want to ask... were you there? This time the burden is mine. Dramatizing the unexpected journey of Henri Matisse, one of the world's most renowned artists, became quite a challenge; please forgive me a few curlicues of poetic license.

The setting is France and beyond. The time, the mid-19th to the mid-20th centuries. A tale of such twists and turns roots itself into a socio-political context. All Europe was headed for the white water rapids of financial meltdown, confronted by the virulent rip-tide of a left-wing backlash. Coalescing as the Paris Commune, the militant resistance was brief and avowedly socialist; it dominated for a mere three months before being overcome by the National Guard. At a conservative estimate over 30,000 Communards were slaughtered with countless more injured.

The Panic of 1873 followed, dragging all global markets into The Long Depression of financial collapse. If you thought the crash of 1929 was 'the big one,' you aren't looking back far enough. What a troubled atmosphere surrounding the young Matisse, making choices that would affect the rest of his life. Against all odds, he usually opted for the more radical options, in his life and his work.

Born near the Belgian border on the last day of December in 1869, he was welcomed by his strict father and indulgent mother, Emile and Anna. Their first son. Her family's money helped build the business from a grain merchants into a local department store. Their unconventional politics allowed her free reign to work as well as raise the children.

Henri was spoiled rotten by his Maman, who turned a forgiving blind eye to his jolly japes and misdemeanours. Following his parents' wishes, he took up articles in a local law firm, but any ambitions to practice were cut short when appendicitis threatened his life. To ease the boredom of his recuperation, his mother bought him a set of paints; it changed him forever.

During the sixty years of his output he escaped the restrictive artistic discipline of the time - copying classical works – instead adopting a series of more contemporary 'isms' including Fauvism, Impressionism, and Primitivism. As well as paintings in various media, his prolific body of work comprises sculpture, printmaking, decoupage, book illustration, and design. In parallel with his fragile family loyalties, he was driven to paint, there was simply no other choice. Every day he found constant inspiration in the sheer joy of colour.

The professional relationship between artist and model often intertwines with their personal lives. Indeed, in his later years, Matisse devoted an entire series to variations on the theme. His own entanglement with Lydia Delectorskaya, a woman forty years his junior, reflected both her own troubled past and his lifelong dilemma. *Woman in a Purple Coat,* the iconic painting of Lydia, only hints at the profound relationship between them, her pose of relaxed abandon also revealing her unique character as an independent woman.

Her volcanic effect on his unconventional marriage exploded their story across the border to melodrama. To the end, he never stopped searching for the precise moment of The Now. The day before he died at the age of 84, Matisse asked for a ball point pen and drew Lydia's portrait. With a final glance he declared, "It will do."

Always open to new forms of representation, Matisse admired cinematic techniques and screen images. My tale parodies a screenplay. Peppered with special effects, imagined flashbacks and flash-forwards, it attempts an amalgam of the scenes and memories that might connect unspoken truths.

The fascinating accounts of Louis Aragon, the poet who befriended Henri, and of biographer Hilary Spurling's meticulous revelations can guide you further. My own effort relies more on creating ambience and emotion. In reality, it can only ever be an impression of Matisse, which I hope would have pleased him.

The Painted Lady

The lights dim in the cinema. Buttery fingers pluck a piece of warm popcorn from its carton. A late-comer slides into an empty aisle seat. The screen becomes infused with a dazzling light as up in the projection booth, a celluloid strip clicks through the sprocket holes. The blare of unseen trumpets, and the film begins. Let the credits and the good times roll!

Based on a true story!

Starring Monsieur Henri Matisse, Multi-Award Winner!

Madame Amélie Parayre Matisse, aka Melo, as you've never seen her before!

And introducing Mam'selle Lydia Nikolaevna Delectorskaya, the ingenue setting tongues a'wag all over France!

Auteur: Mam'selle B. Porter

[The throaty tones of a professional voice artist narrate an introduction over a series of still sepia photographs.]

> Imagine one of those European rail stations, elegant, embodying the architecture of wrought iron and glass. Not merely a place of arrivals and departures, but a metaphor for the era itself. Imagine three tracks meeting in the middle of the station. Trains coming in, trains leaving. One track opens out and accepts another train, coupled to the first. They chug along for a bit, but one of the engines develops a fault, can hardly keep up, and has to be taken out of service. Lifted by crane, deposited on the sidings. It's reinstated but dented and damaged. Then another train seems to collide with those two. Wham! Wallop! Crash!

[Still under a sepia wash, the camera tracks around the small bustling town of Bohain-en-Vermandois, its low-rise shops and houses with their gabled roofs and attic windows. We follow a woman dressed in the finery of the era, albeit slightly out-of-date. She leads a young boy by the hand. He's about nine or ten. As they pass, a small flock of homing pigeons, released from their coops, fly over their heads. The boy tries to reach up to touch them. This is Henri Matisse and his mother Anna.]

Henri: *Je veut voir l' étoffe, Maman, s'il te plait.*

Anna : *Encore*, Henri? Why do you like all those rolls of cloth?

Henri : It's the colours, Maman... so many colours!

[Now he's pulling her along the corridor to a store room of fabrics, as the screen fades to black.

The story continues with a sudden explosion of hard-edged colour, as though lit under fluorescent tubes. Four lads parade around an otherwise quiet bar, grabbing at pints from occupied tables, standing on the bar, singing and declaiming. Annoying monsieur le patron and the customers. Young Henri, now in his teens, is one of the quartet. He waggles his bottom at a middle-aged couple, nursing glasses of wine. When they refuse to acknowledge him, he lowers his trousers and moons them, to the great amusement of his pals.]

> She's so pretty, I'm so witty.
> Here's a ditty, To her titty!
> Absinthe makes the prick grow fonder,
> Makes us wonder what's out yonder.
> But just before you go, you know,
> Pass the booze until we snooze.
> Feeling fine, so pass the wine,
> And pass the beers m'dears;
> There's brandy, Randy-Andy,
> That's music to our ears.
> Fill this glass with Slavic kvass, this one's just for you.
> *Messieurs*, I say, *s'il vous plait*! Time to hit *les rues*!

[Cut to Henri, fully clothed, asleep on top of the covers in his bedroom. His mother shakes his shoulder till he opens his eyes.]

> Anna: Henri, wake up, *mon cher*. You'll be late for work.
>
> Henri: Ooh, I can't, Maman. Feel sick.

Anna: Yes, I heard you rumble in last night like a tank through the village. I daresay everyone heard you.

Henri: No, it hurts. [He points to his right side] Here. It's on fire.

[He falls back onto the pillow, eyes closed. When he opens them he's in a hospital ward. Sparse and white. His mother confers with the doctor at the foot of his bed.]

Doctor: Luckily we caught it in time. Thanks to you, Madame. Quick thinking, if I may say so. If that appendix had burst, well, he's lucky to be alive.

Anna: *Merci, docteur*. When can I take him home?

Doctor: Remember, complete rest. Essential. The nurse will give you a diet regime.

[The camera follows Henri, quite weakened in recovery, as he accompanies his mother through some of the departments of the family general store. Anna's in charge of the handful of women mixing colours in the paint department, each protected by ankle-length work-smocks. She checks on quality against a colour chart of labelled tones. Some of the older women tousle Henri's hair as he walks past, and he flirts with a few of the younger girls, making them laugh.

While his mother is occupied, he wanders into another section, always his favourite. A large cutting table dominates the room, set with high-backed work stools, all currently empty. On display are shelf upon shelf of rolled up fabrics – all materials from the finest voiles, silks and satins to cottons and linens and woven hemp. Each shelf is defined by swatches attached to the rolls. Henri pulls out a metre of voile and peers through it, distorting the lay-out of the room. He's entranced by the boldest colours and patterns, feeling the material between his fingers. The sun pours through the window as he sits down, suddenly feeling weak. As his eyes droop the sunbeam transforms itself, coalescing into a large woman, a huge woman, her head grazing the ceiling, draped in a garment of no known style, a mixture of toga, sari, ballerina skirt, riding jacket, all dazzling and bright.

When he opens his eyes, Anna stands before him, holding a set of paints.]

Anna: Here, *cheri*, this is for you.

[From nowhere and another time comes Henri's voice]

Henri: 'The moment I held the box of colors in my hand I knew this was my life. I threw myself into it like a beast that plunges toward the thing it loves.'

[A quick flash forward to a neat cottage garden, super-imposed through the hospital window, where a few art students in paint-stained smocks are trading some shocking news.]

She's been shot.

Who... Madame?

No, Mam'selle. The model, not the daughter.

What.... What are you talking about?

Shot, in the chest.

That's absurd!

Is she dead?

In the hospital. Touch and go.

Who'd want to shoot her?

She did it herself.

What are you talking about?

[The camera creeps in through the window to another more modest garden, young Matisse seated in front of an easel, trying to conquer the scene in oil paints. Half-hidden in the doorway his sour-faced father watches. He speaks to his son from the shadows.]

Emile: What are you talking about, not going back? We pulled some strings to get you into that law firm, young man. Are you going to make a fool of your mother and me? At least she decorates porcelain plates. Folk like plates. Folk buy plates. Who's going to buy that rubbish... can't tell if it's a rose or a rabbit. [Henri doesn't reply.] Well... what have you got to say for yourself? [Henri concentrates on the painting.] Henri! Dammit!

Henri: Sorry, Papa, what did you say?

[The old man snorts in disgust and calls to his wife before disappearing back inside.]

Emile: Anna! He's like a brick wall. You talk to him!

[Cut to Matisse in front of his easel in a tiny all-purpose room, crowded with a divan, a kitchen table covered with paint tubes and palettes among soiled dishes, a few store cupboards, their open doors revealing salad leaves and apples. A kitten cavorts on the earthen floor which is covered by a carpet, its once-vibrant pattern faded. On a chair, posing for her portrait, is Camille, completely naked, a cloth of green stripes draped across her thigh. She a contemporary of Henri's, both as mischievous and serious as he, and always referred to as Camille, though her given name is Caroline.]

Henri: *Bouge pas, cherie*. I need the light just... there!

Camille: *Oui m'sieur*.

[She sits, he paints. A fly lands on her knee and the cloth slips. She bends to pick it up.]

Henri: NO! I said don't move! Caroline!

Camille: *Monsieur*, you know my name is Camille.

Henri: Cammi, Caro, what's the difference. You're all the same. Here, and here, and here! [Using his paint brush he points to her breasts, her pubic hair, and her mouth. He bends to kiss her, and paints a smear across her cheek.]

Camille: That tickles!

Henri: Oho, it tickles does it. [He carries her over his shoulder to the divan and plagues her with tickles that end in consensual love-making.]

[Cross-fade to almost exactly the same scene, with Matisse in front of his easel, painting Camille, still naked, another cloth across her knee, this one decorated with vine leaves. She is now noticeably pregnant. The cat has grown, as well. The fly buzzes around the room. Very annoying.]

Camille: I need to pee!

Henri: Wait!

Camille: Henri, stop! [She rises, collects a chamber pot from under the divan, and squats to relieve herself.]

Henri: [in mock despair] You are ruining my life, Mam'selle!

[And again, the same scene, but now Camille's pregnancy has almost come to full term. The cloth is wider, a solid slab of red. The cat, no longer a kitten, rubs against Matisse's ankle. Both Camille and the cat sneeze at the same moment, to Henri's great amusement. He bats away the fly.]

Henri: *Eh, bien*, my little musician, I never heard that tune before!

Camille: *Mon cher*, it's freezing in here. And the baby *aussi*, it's kicking up a snowstorm. Feel. [He's been trying to overpaint a bold black line, but has run out of paint.] Come on, take a break.

[Henri sets down his brush and kneels in front of her, placing his ear against her belly.]

Camille: So, have you decided? Are you going to do the decent, or is this kid going to trot through life with no name?

Henri: I hope he won't expect me to play soccer with him.

Camille: Might be a little girl...

[He notices the bucket of burnt charcoal by the stove, grabs a lump, and returns to the painting, dragging the coal down, down, down until he's satisfied with the vertical. The camera pulls out to a very wide shot of the little house, so little it turns into a doll's house, with cut-away frontage. Emile, grumpy as ever, steps up behind the house like a giant, his enormous eye peering into the window. He speaks with the boom of echo-reverb.]

Emile: Don't expect your mother and me to fix this, Henri. She'll only drag you down. You can't even wipe your own ass, let alone support a baby. You found her in the gutter, send her back there, to her own kind.

Camille: I am right here... I can actually hear you!

Henri: Don't worry... I'm taking her to Paris. I have a place at l'Académie Julian.

Emile: And who's going to pay for that, I wonder!

[She hobbles across the room, throws a woolen blanket across her shoulders and prepares some tea. But she drops the kettle down Bang! Contractions have begun.]

Camille: [screaming] Henri!

Henri [with supreme indecision]: Maybe he's right. Fuck it, I don't know what to do for the best...

[Cut to the fly, landing on a plate smeared with egg yolk. It's joined by two more. They fly out the door. But instead of giving birth in Henri's house, Camille pushes the baby into the world lying on a greasy mattress on the ground. Roaches and rats make scurrying sounds, and her screams blend with the urgent cries of a very hungry new-born.

Henri pushes his way through the lanes lined with rubbish. He's racked with guilt. When he finds Camille and the baby, he sinks to his knees, in tears. Exhausted, Camille flashes him a sad smile.]

Camille: Little girl. You won't have to play soccer.

[Cut inside the house. Peeking through the doorway are a middle-aged couple, neighbours. We see them speaking to Henri, but neither he nor we can hear what they say. Inside the room, Camille lies exhausted on the divan, trying to keep warm under a pile of cloths and a flimsy blanket. Sweat dots her forehead. She falls in and out of sleep. On the chair rests a woven Moses basket. The cat jumps into the basket carrying a tiny kitten. Inside are two more kittens; the cat licks them all as they suckle. Henri cuddles his brand-new daughter, rocking her to stop the crying.]

Henri: Shh, shh ma petite Marguerite. Margot, Largo, Cargo, Fargo... Shh. [He calls over to Camille, now deeply asleep.] Cami why won't she stop screaming?

[Cross-fade into Henri and Camille's Paris apartment. She's not well and the baby is hungry. Henri is sketching. A couple appear at the open doorway, joined by another woman, meaty and kind-faced. She unlaces her chemise, takes the baby from Henri, and offers it her breast. Silence at last. Henri sets down the basket on the floor and guides the nursing woman to the chair. He picks up his palette, squeezes out some colours and begins to paint.]

Woman at the door: Henri, she has the 'monia.

Man at the door: Do something, man, before you lose her!

[Elbowing its way between the couple is a transparent figure, and another, wrapped in rags from head to toe. Images of the future.

They barge into the room and lift Camille from the bed, waking her. She reaches out to Henri but his attention is on his child.]

Camille: *Au revoir*, Henri. I'm leaving. The nuns will take me.

Henri: Turn Margot's head more to me. I need the light.

[With the magic of cinema effects, the baby grows into a toddler, running out the door, chasing the fly. They lead us across the garden, as the child, fully animated, climbs onto the back of the insect; they soar over tree-lined hillocks, along the banks of the Seine, and through the Paris suburbs. The fly deposits Marguerite into the grounds of a wonderful late-18th century Neuilly residence concealed in a private park. The shot widens to include a polite wedding bower decorated with flowers. The camera travels along a raised trestle table of guests from the happy couple in the centre, down to the ground where a dozen tables are also full of merry-makers. One is Henri, delighted by his conversation with the woman next to him. Amélie Parayre. In front of her she's placed a beaded reticule; a toy poodle puppy noses up through the opening.]

Henri: That's a strange-looking cat, Mam'selle!

Amélie: Oh, you are funny, *Monsieur*. This is Frou-frou. She's adorable, *n'est-ce pas*? [She nuzzles the puppy's nose.] Yes, you are, *ma caniche*, yes, you are! [She dips her finger into the icing of the half-eaten cake on her plate and gives it to the dog to lick. Little Marguerite sleeps in her basket, which Henri has set down on the grass beside him.] But who's that puppy in your basket?

Henri: I like you, Mam'selle! [He lifts his sleepy daughter and holds her up to Amélie.] This is *ma petite* Marguerite. Margot-Largo.

Amélie: Oh, I didn't realise you... I mean, is she here, your wife?

Henri: No. She's not... available.

[Amélie signals to one of the waiters in attendance.]

Amélie: She's beautiful. But she can't drink champagne. Let's get her some milk, shall we?

Henri: You are a rare flower. I want to paint you. Right here. Right now.

[The fly buzzes back, leading us to the long trestle table of wedding gaiety. The central couple are now Henri and Amélie. They're approached by her father, Armand, who kisses his daughter on the cheek, and holds out his hand to his new son-in-law.]

Armand: Congratulations, Henri!

Henri [downing a flute of champagne]: *Merci*, Armand. And for this wonderful party!

Amélie [holding out her hand for her father's inspection.]: Look, Papa, a real emerald! From your patron, Mrs Humbert. Wasn't that generous!

[They all look down the table at a well-coiffed woman who holds herself with regal bearing. They wave at her, Amélie displaying the ring. The woman waves back as though she were the Queen. Armand kisses Amelie's cheek again, taking his leave.]

Armand: Remember, we expect a houseful of grand-children!

Amélie [indicates Marguerite, who's been playing on the grass.]: Well, you can start with this little terror! Will you come with us to Corsica, little mousey, our honeymoon in the sunnymoon?

[She reaches down to tickle the little giggling girl, then turns to Henri and feeds him a forkful of cake. He pretends to gobble the fork, her hand, and up along her arm. He kisses her passionately on the mouth.]

Amélie: Happy, *mon amour*?

[He gives her a tipsy smile, but slightly hesitates in his reply.]

Amélie: What is it... what can I do to make it better?

Henri: I need a proper teacher. I need to learn. [He stands, shouts to all the guests.] I need to learn!

Amélie [rising from her chair to quiet him]: And so you shall, Henri. [They kiss.] Do you love me?

Henri: I love you dearly, *ma fleur* Melo; but I shall always love painting more.

[Laughing, Amélie reaches for the plate of uneaten cake and shoves it into his face, like a clown's finale.]

Amélie [running around the table to escape him]: You're insufferable, *Monsieur*!

[He splutters, wipes his face, but his glasses are still clogged, his vision blurred. When he tries to throw the cake back at her, it hits four-year-old Marguerite. She joins in the fun, running with Amélie, and pelts Henri with more cake.]

Marguerite: 'Suff'ble! 'Suff'ble, Papa!

[Cut to Henri seated in a semi-circle with fellow students painstakingly trying to bring some originality to their interpretation of various objects laid out on a table. Le Maître, the renowned instructor Gustave Moreau, inspects each canvas, tapping on some with his walking stick.]

Moreau: Enough, enough! *Ça suffit, messieurs. Nom de dieu*!! Brushes down and shut the fuck up. *Ecoutez*! This is serious. Are you children, automatons, are your feet stuck fast to the floor? I have urged you to fly, to soar. To let the paint speak to you, guide you on your own journey. And what do I see? Plod, plod, plod. Did you think I was speaking to the wind, that I'm in love with my own voice? You have come to Paris, you have come to Gustave Moreau. Perhaps it is best if you lay on your bellies and crawl back to the little lives you came from. Go on, out of my sight!

[Moreau turns his back on the students, all men in their twenties who believed he would prepare them for admission to the *Société Nationale des Beaux-Arts.* They shuffle out of the room, whispering their bafflement, anger, disappointment. Henri is among the last to leave.]

Moreau: Matisse! Wait. Come here.

Henri: *Oui, Maître*.

Moreau: I will work with you. There is something, something... something we can build on. Your palette is dark, almost sinister. Fine, provided you know why. Don't be afraid to turn it upside down. Colour can be your friend... if you want it to. I will work with you. You will get elected to the *Société.* And one more thing...

Henri: *Oui*?

Moreau: You must never listen to the taunts of others. Promise me. If they can't see the merits of your work, the problem is in their eyes, not on your canvas.

[Fade to black. Fade up on a wall displaying a selection of paintings by Cézanne. We hear Henri's voice over as the camera pans from canvas to canvas.]

Henri: In modern art, it is to Cézanne that I owe the most. He is the God of painting. Why? The planes of colour, which define light itself. Imagine... capturing light itself. Like an entomologist filling his jar with fireflies! The very essence of colour gives me an energy as if from witchcraft. Yes, I use black... to define, to enlighten, if that's not a contradiction. Black for me is the Queen of Colour! I may be a non-believer, but this is truly divine. Celestial. Just look. An apple, a wall, a nose. The subject is not the subject. Cézanne paints the light, and I, too, must paint the light. Surely an act of a magician. [The wall of Cézannes has become a wall of Matisse nudes.] You ask why I study the nude figure. As though I were a pervert. It is the nude which offers an infinite variety of light across the planes of the flesh. Each model is different, each pose as well. Do you see... exactly the same, yet utterly different. I can never tire of it. Never.

[Fade again to black as the voice-over narrator returns, the dialogue illustrating another series of still sepia photographs. Some depict the Matisse family, but a few reproduce the train station and tracks from the opening scene.]

> By the turn of the twentieth century, the Matisse family had become a cosy unit of five: Work-obsessed Monsieur and doting Madame, their obedient daughter Marguerite, and the two little boys, Jean and Pierre. We will explore more of their domestic lives, I promise, but first, a new twist. Else there wouldn't be much of a story! Remember that train crash? It's time to fuel up a sad and foreign engine, feed it enough to set its wheels spinning thousands of kilometres away, on a collision course to unexpected adventure, pain, and healing. Hear that lonesome whistle blow... toot-toot!

[Cut to a repeat of the scene set in the cottage garden, though from another more intimate angle, featuring the art students in paint-stained smocks.]

She's been shot.

Who... Madame?

No, Mam'selle. The model, not the daughter.

What.... What are you talking about?

Shot, in the chest.

That's absurd!

Is she dead?

In the hospital. Touch and go.

Who'd want to shoot her?

She did it herself.

What are you talking about?

[Here begins a series of silent images as described.

The garden scene closes in on a row of oxeye daisies, the screen a blank except for one flower's golden eye; this begins a succession of images of a spinning newspaper, a familiar cinematic technique to introduce important news. Each image grows from a central point to fill the entire screen. All are headed with the date 23 June.

The first image resolves to a disembodied hand wielding a chisel on a stone stele reading: Ptolemy XV Egyptian Pharaoh. The hand pushes too hard on the tool, and the image cracks into pieces and falls off the screen. The hand turns red with embarrassment, drops the chisel, and backs off to one side. It is replaced by a succession of three newspaper front pages of birth announcements… names and short descriptions: Joséphine de Beauharnais, wife of Napoleon I; Edward VIII, King of England; and finally Jean Anouilh, French dramatist. But the disembodied hand sneaks onto the screen and rips down Anouilh's headline, hastily replacing it with an announcement of the birth of Lydia Nikolaevna Delectorskaya, companion to Henri Matisse. The hand makes the universal gesture 'OK' and proudly struts off-screen.

Cut to an old-fashioned illustrated map of Tsarist Russia, neat line drawings mark key cities, rivers, borders, the landscape covered in snow. Footprints appear, but without anyone to make them. As they trudge north, the snow gradually melts away. The map highlights the Siberian border, and closes in on the city of Tomsk. The map reverts to a highly stylised gouache painting of the streets, the administrative stone headquarters, the lanes of shops opening out into a well-stocked produce market, and the wooden residences decorated with gingerbread-type frieses. The camera finds a tidy path off the road, leading to a two-storey house in typical rural Siberian style. The flowers and shrubs of summer beckon us further. Painted on the post-box outside are the words Doctor Nikolai Delectorskaya, Pediatrician, written in the Cyrillic alphabet; the phrase morphs into English. We creep inside a large ground floor window into a well-appointed apartment.

This begins a series of transition images, each lasting a few moments but still onscreen when the next appears. Each fading shot propels us forwards in time. These include a doctor clamping a baby girl's umbilical cord and slapping her bottom to produce a cry… to the delight of the new mother; the little girl at a table, flanked by her parents, lifted up by her father to blow out three candles on a beautifully iced cake… amid praise from them, she snuggles happily into her father's embrace; the family watching from the window as a line of soldiers marches out of town, dressed in uniforms of World War I; Lydia's mother chooses a head of cabbage from a market stall as she leads her father by the hand to buy a bouquet… she's happy, she hugs him; even aged eight she's quite a little beauty… deep blue eyes, blond wavy hair dressed in the long braids of Slavic tradition.

Cut to Lydia aged ten and freed from her lessons, running with a couple of classmates from the school along the River Tom. She waves goodbye to her friends, turns into the grounds of a medical complex. She stops before a pale low-lying maternity hospital. The entrance is guarded by a granite plinth displaying a bizarre metal sculpture of a new-born baby emerging from the leaves of a cabbage… though for audiences in the know, it's a sculpture yet to come. A satiric comment on the traditional fairy-tale that babies come from the cabbage patch. As Lydia reaches out to the statue, it disappears beneath her hand.

She skips into the building and through its clean marbled corridors, exchanging greetings with some uniformed nurses and other staff. She knows her way to a ward of pregnant women. She joins a group of pediatric students being led by her father. He smiles, carrying on with his rounds. Everyone accepts her right to be there. Along with the other students, young Lydia writes down her father's words in a small notebook.

Cut to another bed in another ward. Lydia's mother, face covered in sweat, lies motionless as two masked attendants cover her in a shroud, lift her onto a trolly and wheel her away.

Cut back to the family apartment, but the mother is missing. It's the same table and a similar birthday cake, this time with twelve candles. When Lydia blows them all out, the screen goes black.

Over the blackness we hear the mournful strains of Chopin's Funeral March. Fade up to a graveyard where Lydia is being comforted by relatives and neighbours. One is a woman resembling her mother, and is in fact her younger sister, the epitome of an "earth mother." She embraces her niece, surrounded by three of her own children, one a similar age to Lydia, the other two several years younger.]

Lydia [through her sobs, leaning against her Aunt]: He always called me his *kotyonok*, his little kitten. Remember, Auntie? He said I could be a doctor, just like him. He promised. He promised.

Aunt: Shh, malyshka. Come with us, we'll look after you. Won't we, children? Shh.

Lydia: I saw it. On the ward... cholera ... I saw it. Smelled like fish and everyone wanted water. But all the typhus wards were in the main hospital, where they took Mamochka. When I'm a doctor I'll find a cure, I will!

Aunt: [now also in tears] You're such a good girl.

Lydia: Don't cry, Auntie. I'll do it!

Aunt: We have to get out of here, little one. It's not safe.

Lydia: Out of the cemetery?

Aunt: No, out of Tomsk. We have to take a train. That will be exciting, won't it?

Lydia: Where are we going?

Aunt: China.

[A screen caption announces it is Four Years Later, Harbin, China. Cut to a Manchurian apartment house, looking remarkably like the architecture of Tomsk. Inside Lydia sits at a table covered in books;

her eldest cousin studies with her. The two little ones have made a fort of blankets, peeking out occasionally. Lydia's Aunt can be seen in the kitchen, through an archway, preparing soup on a stove. Lydia's braids have gone, replaced by a shoulder-length bob, showing off her wavy hair, more suitable for a sixteen-year-old.]

Aunt [calling the children from the kitchen] Clear the table, now, my darlings. The soup's ready. [Lydia is obedient, but interrupted by a knock on the door.] Can you get that, malyshka, it's Valeria Ivanova, you remember, from Tomsk.

[Cut to everyone around the table, each with a soup bowl, using chop sticks to dip boiled dumplings into the fragrant liquid. They're joined by Mrs Lan, an elderly Manchurian woman, her flat eye-lids revealing Mongolian ancestry. A tame pigeon perches on her head, very well behaved but prone to squawking when the conversation becomes too animated. Mrs Lan speaks quickly, with her mouth full, chattering away. Neither Lydia nor her Aunt understands a word, but they nod. They don't want to be disrespectful.

Lydia [half-whispers to her cousin] How will I ever learn this language if they speak so quickly! [He tweaks her nose with his chopsticks. They suppress their giggles. When the woman pauses to sip some tea, Valeria translates.]

Valeria: She says she's heard from her son, the one who moved far away to be in the sunshine. France. Too cold for him here. [she mimes shivering]

[Mrs Lan imitates her, laughing. The pigeon fluffs up its feathers. She carries on with her story.]

Valeria: Now she's cursing him, says he thinks he's a Mongol emperor, does whatever he wants, and he's left her here to fade away. Like the spring snow. [They all listen to the woman. Then Valeria bursts out laughing.] She says, he might as well take a dagger and stick it in her heart! [Mrs Lan pretends to stab herself in the chest with a chopstick; she slumps onto the table, miming her death throes. It's clear she has the precise timing of an experienced comedienne, and they all laugh with her.]

Lydia: Actually, Auntie, I've been thinking we might go to France. Not the cold, but, you know, take my chances at getting into the Sorbonne. What do you think, Valeria Ivanova?

Valeria: Oh, well... yes... Da! Da!... Yes, we have Siberian friends all over France. Paris, the Riviera. But there's no hurry, is there? She's such a serious girl!

Aunt: My burden and my joy! [she kisses her niece on the cheek, as Mrs Lan resumes her chatter through slurped soup.]

Valeria: Mrs Lan says if you're determined to go to Paris you have to get the train to Moscow, and then… [she hesitates]… then…

Lydia: Then what?

Valeria: Then you take your life in your hands!

[Cut to an aerial shot. Loitering and farewells at the Harbin railroad station. Destinations heading west across into Russia, eastward to the docks, and far south crossing into Korea. The camera tracks across seven quays, before settling near a departure sign for Moscow. The shot levels out, closing along the crowded open-air platform, passengers and well-wishers are frozen in time, as though caught in a photograph: three western men wearing straw boaters chat with the guard, checking the time on the station clock-tower; a Chinese woman, dressed in a wide-sleeved over-jacket decorated with flowered bands around the hem, hides her faces behind a huge paper fan. She stands alongside two Manchu men, father and son. They compare bits of paper, each wearing dark silk tunics over ankle-length skirts, their hair hidden under skull-caps except for the long single braid down their backs. The younger man carries a small child on his shoulders, cheeks glowing with cold.

The child's cheeks turn red, and his breath is visible as the scene reverts to live action, hustle and bustle along the platform. Lydia, her Aunt and cousins, are being fussed over by Valeria Ivanovna and other neighbours, lots of hugs and parcels of food for the journey. Information signs are in Russian and French, as well as Manchu and Mandarin. Waiting on the rails, the powerful presence of a steam locomotive snorts warning puffs into the air. Three Buddhist nuns in full-length saffron robes rush past Lydia, gabbling to each other in French. Lydia and her relatives climb into a third-class carriage, settling into straight-backed window seats. The whistle blows and blows again. The engine chugs slowly, then gains speed. The crowds on the platform shrink to the size of little beetles, scurrying after the train.

The screen fills with clouds of grey steam from the locomotive's smoke-stack. It clears to reveal a small study room, part of an academic library. Lydia, dressed in a calf-length grey serge pinafore, is the only occupant; she sits at the table writing in a thick journal. A window above provides her daylight. We hear her voice over as she writes. Her words appear onscreen in translation, phrases picked out from the pages of the book. Her face is also superimposed in extreme close-up, sometimes paused in thought, and a few times along with animated thought-bubbles as she drags memories back from her early life.]

Lydia: So, here I am at last! I think you'd be proud of me, Papa. The Sorbonne. Remember we used to speak about it? As if it were just one building. I had no idea it was spread out all over Paris like mushrooms. I'm glad you and Mamochka forced me to study French at the gymnasium in Tomsk, or else I wouldn't even be able to buy a coffee and croissant for breakfast! Then I'd starve and then where would we be.

I miss you so much, Papa, Mamochka too, of course, and I want to succeed, especially for you. Auntie and the cousins have been very kind. They really take good care of me. And if you remember her soup you'll know there's no chance of starving. A three-course meal in a tiny bowl!

Auntie found us a place in the quartier they call Little Siberia, quite a welcome touch of home. I do feel guilty... they've sacrificed everything for me. I'm sure I don't deserve it. The old folk have come down here to make sure their children have a good future, but I think it takes their toll. Uprooted like that. Remember how we used to re-pot those plants, and some just didn't make it, no matter how careful we were with the soil and water.

We're squeezed into two small rooms near l'hôpital Bicêtre where the faculty takes all the maternity course work. I've only been here for a few days, but I'm learning so much. Especially about the hospital itself. What a history! One of my lecture-mates was so funny... she acted out all the transformations as if she were performing at the Folies Bergère. She says it was a converted gunpowder factory, then a refuge for homeless women, then a prison for prostitutes, and finally a general holding pen for all the pitiful demented folk. Did you know that some of the staff back then thought it was fine to charge people to come to the asylum and laugh at the lunatics?

It made me cry, Papa. I remember when you took me on your rounds, and there were some soldiers, prisoners from the war with Prussia, but you said it was 'our duty to heal no matter who the patient was, friend or foe.' You were truly the best person in all the world.

Now, some news, but I'm not sure whether it's good or not. I've been summoned to the administrative office in a few days. I don't mind admitting I'm nervous, but Auntie said she'd come with me.

[Cut to Lydia and her Aunt in the Paris flat. Lydia is sobbing her heart out, and there's not much Auntie can do to comfort her, except for hugs and soothing words of love. After a while, Lydia pulls away, confused but trying desperately to offer solutions.]

Lydia: I just can't understand. They already accepted me. I'm enrolled in all the courses. All the paperwork.

Auntie: I know, darling, but if they say you're not French, then you're not French. And, they're right, you're not.

Lydia: But they know I can't afford those fees. Whether I was born in France or on the moon. It's not fair!

Aunt: Maybe if we asked around, you know, in Little Siberia... your cousin already knows some of his work mates. Good blokes... even the French ones!

Lydia: Oh, dear Auntie, you're as kind as Papa, but they hardly have enough money for themselves, let alone any for me. Anyway, most of them think a woman studying is a sin against nature.

Aunt: Well, maybe we should try a different kind of plan.

Lydia: What do you mean?

[Cut to a large clock filling the screen, its hands running backwards over the Roman numerals. The hands spin faster, finally stopping at seconds before midnight. As the clock strikes, a caption is superimposed on the screen: **1902 The Humbert Affair.**

This scene is played out in the exaggerated style of a silent melodrama of the era. Black and white. Stilted movement of the actors. Over-enthusiastic make-up borrowed from theatrical productions lit by footlights. Just visible at the bottom right of the screen is a piano player, improvising accompaniment.

The setting is a spacious office. Mrs Humbert, slumps behind the large desk dividing the room. When she lifts her head, we recognise her from the Matisse wedding. Seated on one chair opposite is Amélie's mother, in tears. Her husband, Armand stands beside her, his arm around her shoulder; he stares disbelieving at the woman behind the desk. Henri's mother Anna sits in the other chair, trying to keep her dignity; Emile's hand rests stiffly on her shoulder. Deep lines of greasepaint pencil are etched onto their weary faces. Henri stands at the side, shaking his fist in fury.

The screen cuts to a written caption of explanation, flickering like those of a silent movie: **Painter Matisse caught in scandal. Fraud victims face total ruin. Murder suspected.**

Fade up on the interior of a millinery shop, the shelves tastefully displaying hats of bright colours and contemporary styles. Amélie tries not to show her dismay as she presides over two uniformed officials who remove all the hats, packing them into boxes, and carrying them outside to a waiting carriage. Pierre, her two-year-old toddler thinks everything is a big game. She's speaking with Emile, gabbling, trying desperately to figure out some answers.]

Amélie: *C'est ça, monsieur*, this is me finished! If I'm left with one eyelash I don't even have another to make a pair! The shop is gone. Our apartment on *rue de Châteaudun*… you know we're being evicted. This isn't Henri's doing, *monsieur*.

Emile: I know, my dear. Who'd have suspected that woman could be so devious?

Amélie: Devious… she's a monster from hell! Armand, my father, this will kill him. We're not the only ones.

Emile: I know... Anna can't take much more. *Attends*... I have an idea. Where's Henri just now?

Amélie: Looking after Jean and Marguerite, packing up the flat... unless he's been captured by a paint brush!

Emile: What did he ever do to deserve you, Madame?! Now, listen carefully...

[Cut to the Matisses' apartment, amid the chaos of packing and domestics. Emile faces his son and daughter-in-law at the table.]

Amélie [conflating tears and anger]: What a bitch... she's ruined so many people. She said she believed in him, my father. He wanted to start a newspaper... *Avenir de Seine et Marne... L'Avenir*, the Future! She gave him the money. Gave him the money! We were convinced she was as free-thinking as we are. Henri... say something.

Emile: He's a trained lawyer.

Henri: Yes, yes, of course, Papa, I will help. He needs a good defense. We can't trust the courts.

Emile: How long can you stay here before they kick you out? We can take a corner and make an office. Marguerite, are you good at copying?

Amélie: And you're sure this will help my father?

Emile [inviting a response to his chant]: *Allons-y Alonzo!* All for one...

[They all reply] And one for all!

[Fade to black. Fade up on a rapid series of preparations for the trial, mostly featuring Henri:

- studying documents as he gulps coffee,
- questioning the victims of the fraud,
- running up and down stairs,
- knocking on doors,
- walking briskly along the Seine, his bowler hat blown off by the wind, chasing after it, but having to stop to catch his breath,

- Henri and his family seated at gunpoint as the police raid the studio for 'evidence,'
- grabbing some food put down by Amélie, but leaving it unfinished as he dashes out again.

Fade again to black, and fade up into daylight. The Ile de la Cité in the middle of the Seine. Close in on the imposing façade of the Palace of Justice. The camera creeps into the enormous lobby.

Henri appears from the floor above and leads the defendants down the steps. Supporters crowd the lobby, some draped in the French flag. The sound of cheering drowns out any dialogue. As Henri reaches the bottom step he staggers, clutches at his heart and falls to the ground. Marguerite, Amélie, and her parents rush to him. The scene grinds into slow-motion as a doctor's voice takes over the sound track.]

Doctor: Total exhaustion. The body cannot take it. Leave the city, get him into the fresh air. But rest. Above all, total rest. At least two months. Better with five. Unless you'd prefer a funeral.

[Cut to a glaring white screen. From the far right corner, our old friend the fly buzzes in a straight line, landing on a tiny spot in the centre. It grows and grows to reveal Amélie, after her bath, posing naked for Henri. She dries herself with a small white towel. She lowers the towel and walks around to examine the painting.]

Amélie: Let me see, *cheri*, you haven't had a break for hours. I'm starving if you're not!

[Henri is still not on top form, but he welcomes his wife with an arm around her waist.]

Amélie: [with mock surprise, disapproval] What are those meant to be? [she's pointing to her feet in the picture.]

Henri: What?

Amélie: Are you turning me into *un phoque*, a seal? Those are not feet, they're flippers!

Henri: I'll flip you right on your head, Madame! [He tries to lift her onto the bed, but he's too weak. Amélie is immediately concerned, but wants to be positive.]

Amélie: I'm not sure I should pose for you anymore. At least not in the nude. I'm so fat after Pierre's birth.

[Henri buries his face against her belly.]

Henri: Come here, my little *phoque*, while I eat you all up!

[Amélie calls through to the kitchen.]

Amélie: Marguerite! Is there any tea for us peasants?

[Fade out and back up again onto a superimposed caption reading 'some years later.' Marguerite waits for Amélie to emerge from the wash room. She wears a loose-fitting robe. Further back into the main studio room is a suitcase underneath the open window.]

Marguerite: *Bonjour*, Maman. Have you just had a wash, or are you posing.

Amélie: I think my posing days are over, darling. You'll have to sit in for me even more.

Marguerite: I've always loved that robe.

Amélie: So does your father. I wish we could go with him. Imagine... the whole family creeping through the jungle. Gauguin's letter promises fishing boats just outside his hut, everyone sleeping naked on the beach, sunsets in scarlet and gold. Like the birds. Henri loves birds.

[Marguerite pretends to be a bird, flying around the room, chirping and squawking. Amelie laughs, but breathes in sharply at the stitch in her side.]

Marguerite: Maybe we could stowaway. Empty out that suitcase and fold ourselves inside!

Amélie: People used to call us The Inseparables... now we're scattered to the four corners.

Marguerite: Well, I'd like to train somewhere as a dress designer, but you know I've always loved helping with the boys.

Amélie: Oh, my little Margot-Largo, you're like my right hand.

Marguerite: And we both know how grumpy *Grandpere* Matisse can be, but Jean adores him, *Grandmere* Anna, too. And if your sister Berthe could adopt little Pierre he'd be the happiest baby in France, our *petit* Peepee!

[It's hard to tell whether Amélie stumbles because of the emotional impact of her daughter's words, or something more physical. But Marguerite is worried.]

Marguerite: Maman!

Amélie: *N'inquiete pas, cherie*. Just a little wobble.

Marguerite: We're getting you a nurse. Soon as possible. Don't even say a word!

[The whole scene physically moves to the right hand side of the screen, which is now split in two. The scene on the right continues, but silently, while on the other side a caption appears over an image of Little Siberia in Paris. It reads Another Option. The scene comes to life as Lydia, almost radiant in her finery, is embraced by a man, his back to us. As her face appears over his shoulder, we see her hesitance, even regret. The scene pulls out to the street outside an official registry office. There are the Aunt, her children, and a few well-wishers we don't recognise. They throw flower petals that land on the couple, sticking to Lydia's hair. Good wishes accompany the flowers, spoken in French and Russian.

The screen splits further into quarters; it keeps sub-dividing. There's a cacophony of dialogue, which resolves into the Voice of the Auteur.]

Auteur: Now that you have a convincing cushion of the main characters, it's about time you heard directly from me. Play in the serious documentary theme music, please, for Talking Heads. Defying our modus operandum using appropriate film techniques, let's project into the future. How exciting is that?! On the armrest of your seat is a keypad. Whenever you see that screen full of head shots, just choose the one that's lit up and press the corresponding button. *Et voila*! I'll conduct an interview with that person. Just for you. I suppose we should begin with the man himself. Here he is talking about his models.

[The screen reverts to an extreme close up of the 40-year-old Matisse, bearded, confident, at ease. As the interview proceeds, the shots become even closer… an eyeball, a nostril, an earlobe, etc. The Auteur remains unseen.]

Auteur: Thank you for agreeing to this interview, Monsieur Matisse. Before we talk Art, can you put paid to those salacious rumours that you have a fetish for women's clothes. And if you're not a cross-dresser, please explain why you kept a closet in your studio filled with dresses and costumes for your models to pose in?

Matisse [speaking quite formally]: Like all artists, painters, writers, composers... we must not merely reflect. We must be the slaves to our ego, become control freaks, recreate the world we need to see. At the same time we must throw off a sense of self, sacrifice it on the more immortal altar of Art itself. [Suddenly he laughs, as though getting the punchline of a joke.] Oh, I see! You want to know if I get a hard-on when I paint them. Listen, honey... I dress my models to help me control what I want you to see. Like a movie director.

Auteur: Right, yes... Uhm... We know you painted many portraits, both of men and women, strangers and friends, none of whom had to play dress up for you. So please explain how those differ from the paintings of your succession of models.

Matisse: Well, some of them were so sophisticated, but some were like little girls... they loved playing dress-up. Like my own daughter. In fact, both Amélie and I treated all the models as family, working partners in Art. The human figures are a crucial part, never like extras in an interior. They are the main theme of my work. I depend absolutely on my model... The model for me is a touchstone, it is a door which I must break open in order to reach the garden, that place where I can be alone and feel good. So even the model exists only for what use I can make of it. Within the work.

Auteur: Okay, I get that. Of course, as you know, there is much speculation about whether or not those models didn't merely pose for you, but became even more intimate.

Matisse [with deep laughter]: That's a matter of record... but unless my dick was an in-and-out thing in the Sex Olympics... my attention was on the paint. Seems you're rather obsessed, Mam'selle. So *faites attention*! This is how I spend each day: I'm up, washed and dressed well before five. After breakfast I walk to my studio and work in the morning light, working, working non-stop until lunch, a simple repast, followed by another work session, sometimes drawing at the local art school, or visiting Monsieur Renoir up the road. A neighbour like that... one must take advantage. And he liked my work, he understood, even though it was so different from his. Yes, I love Cézanne, and I also love Renoir, and you know what, Mam'selle... I don't have to choose one or the other. But I was telling you about my day. After my walk home, I wind down with some violin practice, before my usual supper of vegetable soup, two hard-boiled eggs, salad and a glass of wine. I'm asleep by nine. So just when you imagine I might have time for...

Auteur: I'm just trying to understand. So, would it be true to say, then, that you yourself gained comfort from it, the paint I mean, as well as bringing comfort to those of us who take delight in your images?

Matisse: I want you to ask yourself, Mam'selle... given that so many artworks survive from hundreds of years ago, even more... what is the intent of the artist in depicting a subject that narrates the story of ancient myth? They were mighty explicit, those Greeks and Romans, weren't they? A god becomes a swan or a cloud of fog, and embraces a nude woman. You can bet he's not just giving her cooking lessons, *n'est-ce pas*? Not to mention the Bible tales of a naked woman in the pose of a nursing mother, baby Jesus at her tit. Or those statues of nude men by sculptors who might take a fancy to their models... shock horror! Why are those considered masterpieces, but images of nude models without stories regarded as pornography? What do you say to that?

Auteur: Of course, they're all bodies. Surely you can't deny that nudity stimulates...

Matisse: What... a hard-on, a wetness between the legs? Are you saying that the islanders I saw in the Pacific spend their days and nights having orgies? They don't catch fish, or make music, or repair their huts after a storm?

Auteur: No, no, of course not!

Matisse: Actually it's not the best example. Their customs are so different from ours. In fact sex is a gift... well, a gift for men using women to be unwrapped.

Auteur: Not sure I understand... What do you mean?

Matisse: If a man is owed a favour he's invited to sleep with the daughter, or even the wife. But otherwise they're so strict, so absorbed by the lessons of the Catholic missionaries, they can't even imagine women wearing only swim suits on the beach, or keeping their arms uncovered in public. Still, I think my point is...

Auteur: Oh, I don't know... but I'd still like to hear what effect you'd like your work to bring us.

Matisse: No, pay attention. Please. What I dream of is an art of balance, purity and serenity, devoid of troubling or depressing subject matter, a soothing, calming influence on the mind, something like a good armchair which provides relaxation from physical fatigue. [The shot pulls out so that Henri, in full figure, sinks down into a plush armchair, upholstered in the vine fabric.]

The Auteur [still in voice-over] We will return to this series of talking head interviews. But first sit back and enjoy a little parody of the late, great Busby Berkeley.

[Cut to Henri and Marguerite at the cinema, watching a Busby Berkeley musical number. They're sharing a paper cone of sweets. The camera, mounted on a crane, shoots from overhead to a sound stage where dancers, each one holding a painting, lie on their backs to form a giant flower. The camera swoops down as the women stand. The paintings now appear to have grown legs. A transparent screen drops from the rafters, taking up most of the length of the stage. The women are caught in a rain-shower and run behind the screen for shelter; as the lights change, they appear in silhouette. Marguerite is delighted at the effects and turns to Henri. But he's asleep in his seat.

Henri's dream is accompanied by an orchestral version of the song *She*, made popular by a number of French singers, notably Charles Aznavour. In a parody of Busby Berkeley's famous routine, the silhouetted women undress from their wet clothes. They follow each other from behind the screen, parading with paintings of the many models painted by Henri over the decades. As each passes the camera, the name of the model is superimposed on the screen, and announced by the voice-over of the narrator in the style of an off-screen announcer at a beauty pageant.]

Narrator:

- **Camille Joblaud**, once his great support, she never forgave him for abandoning her in her hour of need, leaving him their daughter Marguerite to raise and living out her years in the care of nuns.
- **Marguerite Matisse**, sometimes known as Margot, Henri's devoted daughter and one of his favourite and most painted models. She and her art critic husband Georges Duthuit had a son, Claude.
- **Amélie Parayre Matisse**, Henri's wife and adored model, whom he affectionately referred to as Melo, and who left him after a lifetime of support through thick and thin; mother to his two sons Jean Gerard and Pierre, she also raised Marguerite as though she were her own child.
- **Bevilacqua**, a dark-haired Italian who posed early on for Henri's sculptures.
- **Carmelita,** another favourite with the dark Mediterranean features he preferred.
- **Lysette Löwengard,** 17 year old daughter of friends of the Matisse family who cared for Henri and Amélie as well as modeling.
- **Louise Brouty**, known affectionately as **Loulou.** She spent a whole summer with the Matisses in a remote Mediterranean fishing village in 1909. Everyone liked her, especially Marguerite and the boys Jean and Pierre. In addition to modeling for Henri and the pupils studying at his new Academy, she became a valued companion for Amélie, whose health was getting worse. When she wasn't posing Henri taught her to swim. By summer's end she'd become so

tanned that Henri's students nicknamed her "the Italian sunset."

- Henri's model as well as his student**, Olga Meerson** fell obsessively in love with him, prompting Amelie's jealousy and doubts about their marriage. Henri's rejection of her ended in tragedy when she departed for Germany and committed suicide.
- **Zorah** provided just the degree of North African ethnicity Henri required for variations on the theme of the Odalisque.
- **Laurette** who posed, sometimes with her sister, over several years for at least fifty of Henri's portraits. She was often dressed in green, sometimes with her black hair peeping out from under a patterned turban. Pierre Matisse remembers her as totally uninhibited, standing naked at the open window for some air, attracting the attention of officers in the police station opposite.
- **Greta Moll** who reacted violently at her body being distorted in Henri's paintings.
- **Antoinette Arnoud,** still a teenager when she posed in the hotel room he'd converted into a studio. She loved the idea of playing dress-up, endlessly trying-on hats for Henri.
- **Henriette Darricarrère** whom Henri discovered working as a film extra at the Studios de la Victorine in Nice. She had studied ballet and was a musician, but Henri was fascinated with the way that light seemed to bounce off her body. She spent seven years posing for him, and was another model tacitly adopted by Amelie. For Henri, who gave her painting lessons, she was the prime inspiration for his series of Odalisque studies.
- **Pauline** a Tahitian native initially sent as Henri's guide by the state authority to encourage tourism, she became his platonic friend and on several occasions his model.

- **Jeanne Vaderin,** whom Henri called Jeannette, is posed behind a table containing two pots each planted with three stems of pink tulips. She's the subject of several Henri's paintings, sculptures and drawings.
- **Micaela Avogadro** was photographed by Henri Cartier-Bresson for an exhibition catalog; Matisse designed the cover. The photo shows his back as he paints. Micaela wears a tartan ball-gown, pulled down so her breasts spill over the dress. Her shoulders are wrapped with a fur stole, and her hair hangs loose save for an almost comic pompadour atop her head. She smiles toothily at Henri. A large wall hanging of Chinese figures overlooks the scene.
- And then, in the midst of WWII, Henri once again suffered the agony of kidney and stomach pain. **Monique Bourgeois,** applied to be his temporary night nurse. Though he was in the final decade of his life, their friendship set him on a new course.

[Once again the screen fills with a patchwork of tiny images, one prominently lit up. The voice over of the Auteur takes over, as the small image widens out to fill the screen in extreme close up.]

Auteur: Press the button on your armrest, you remember, like last time. [The Auteur address Monique.] Now, just relax, no trick questions, I promise. We've met you as Monique Bourgeois, a trained nurse, but you have another name, is that true?

Sister Jacques-Marie: Yes, for most of my life I was a Dominican nun, Sister Jacque-Marie. It was the name I was given upon taking my vows.

Auteur: You only spent a fortnight as night nurse to Matisse, but it's said you knew him as well as anyone bar his family. Why is that?

Sister J-M: I was by his side when he couldn't sleep for the pain. Which was most of the time. I prepared cups of soothing tea, and we sat for hours. Talking, not talking. He wanted to know all about my early life, travelling around with a military family, and his pain seemed less when he dug out stories of his own early life. He admitted that sometimes the pain was so bad that even Madame Matisse said he was turning into a monster. Of course, by then they were living separate lives... though they still wrote to each other nearly every day. He told me many stories, but I was never shocked by them. Very shocking, I assure you! We often laughed together, until it brought on a coughing fit.

Auteur: Is it true you received a scholarship to continue your nursing studies? Was that Matisse's influence?

Sister J-M: I hope you're not implying what you might be implying, Mam'selle. No, the scholarship was awarded on merit... and my determination. I visited him sometimes if I had the time. But Henri was more than generous; he knew money was tight so he offered to pay me to pose for him. Four paintings I recall, and some drawings, charcoal, pencil. I had to wear certain clothes... he told Lydia and she gave them to me to put on. He knew I wanted to improve my own painting technique, and he was very supportive.

Auteur: And yet, you opted to become a novitiate in the Dominican order taking your vows in the convent at Vence.

Sister J-M: Yes, September 1944. Just a year after the Germans occupied Nice. My father was being treated in Vence. [She's holding back the tears.] It's where he's buried. I didn't see Henri for nearly two years.

Auteur: And then, by coincidence, you joined forces. That was a life-changer, *n'est-ce pas*?

Sister J-M: *Oui*. The plan was to rebuild and refurbish the convent's Chapel of the Rosary. I'm sure neither of us could foretell how the design of a rural French chapel would be the gossip of the demi-monde and chattering classes... not to mention smears by clergy in my own order!

[Cut to various images of the interior walls and stained glass windows of the chapel, the huge evocative shapes cut from brightly coloured paper. And the Auteur's voice over taking up the narrative.]

Auteur: It was a controversial project that became the focus of Henri's last decade of life… one that revived his flagging reputation around the world. The atheist and the nun. And all under the supervision of Lydia Delectorskaya, still there, still loyal, still in charge.

[Cut to a chase by a group of doctors, nurses and other medical staff running after Henri, then changing direction to chase Amélie, Marguerite, and finally Jean Matisse. The action is speeded up and the whole sequence is an homage to the Keystone Kops. It is narrated in voice over.]

Narrator: No one wants to make light of the selfless dedication of those healers serving the medical profession, and no one wants to trivialize the serious conditions which they treat. But during their lives, the Matisse family was plagued both by so much physical and mental illness, it must at times have felt like they were being pursued by the entire health service in a comedy routine.

[Cut to black. Gently at first, then with greater ferocity, snow begins to fall against the blackness. Through the flakes and far off into the distance, we can see flares of explosions and gunshots, the angry exchange of war. German bombers rain down their terror along the Channel coast. In the confusion of the storm, Henri takes shelter in an uncomfortable, cold, dank hotel in Marseilles. The snowflakes try to stick to the window pane, but melt on landing and run down in rivulets. He has summoned a lowly member of the hotel staff and irrationally berates him in his rage.]

Henri: Four days! Four days to see my own son. I put up with that sad excuse for a train journey from Paris, overnight, impossible to sleep, slops for coffee. France used to take pride… but since this blasted occupation... What kind of military is this? I'm his father. They have all the documents. He's a mechanic at the Istre airfield, not some spy. Istre… What's that, not even fifty kilometres. If I weren't so ill myself I'd walk there. You must know what's going on. You could requisition a hotel car. A bus. Well, what have you got to say?

Hotel worker: I... don't know what to say, M'sieur. I'm so sorry.

Henri: Perhaps you're working for the enemy... what do you say to that?!

[Another hotel worker joins the first in the doorway; he's out of breath, but hands a sheet of paper to Henri. It bears an official seal. Henri reads it, or rather he devours it!]

Henri: At last! At fucking last!

[Cut to Jean's barracks in Istres. Henri struts around the filthy quarters, slush and mud underfoot. Some of the men gnaw at crusts of stale bread, avidly saving any crumbs that fall from their lips. Henri is horrified by the conditions. He sits on his son's rock-hard cot.]

Henri: You're so thin, *mon fils*. What do they feed you?

Jean: Not much, Papa. [He tries to make light of his condition.] Maman wouldn't be very pleased.

Henri: I'm glad I wouldn't let her come...

Jean: Aunt Berthe said she was ill. Are you looking after her?

Henri: We've hired nurses, companions. Don't worry yourself.

Jean: And Marguerite? And my baby bother?

Henri: I need a piss. Where are the latrines?

Jean: You're joking, aren't you. There's a stream out back. We can do our business, if we can make it through the mud. And whoopie, we're allowed to wash there once a week... if we're strong enough to break the ice on the surface.

[Henri is enraged, but overcome with a powerful affection for Jean. He embraces him, tears in his eyes. His first born son.]

Henri: Pack something. They're letting me take you to Marseilles. Letting me – imagine! Twenty-four hour pass. What a time we'll have.

Jean [daring this question]: Why, Papa? Why did you send us away... what did we do wrong, Pierre and me? [He can't stop the tears, dammed up for decades.]

Henri: *Non, non... pas de tout... c'est pas ça!* We were together *tous ensemble.* Remember? We went riding, we spent lovely evenings while our Margot-Largo read to us. Listening to Pierre play the piano.

Jean: Papa, he hated practicing that piano!

Henri: *De tout façon*, it was the noise. I need total silence to paint. You know that. You were little boys. Little boys make noise. *C'est normal ça*.

Jean [not quite convinced] But Marguerite, she stayed with you.

Henri: Yes, she needed your Maman, she was only a baby. She's always been my loyal model. From the first. Have you seen that bas relief I chiseled of her profile, chubby cheeks, just testing her little legs...

Jean: It's always about you, Papa, isn't it? And still, we love you. We all love you. Why is that?

Henri: Because, look at me, I'm very loveable! [They share a laugh.] Now, come on, give me a hug and let's show the world our Matisse smile. We're off to Marseilles and fuck anyone who gets in our way!

[Cut to Henri and Jean slogging through the freezing mud on their way to the train station. This reverts to a reprise of the Keystone Kops chase. On the soundtrack we hear first one hacking cough, then another, and more until it sounds like an entire bronchitis ward. It's all silenced by the imperious pronouncement of a doctor's voice.]

Doctor: Definitely bronchitis. Only one cure. Get him to the sun. Quick as you can. The Riviera... Nice. Sun and rest. Just do it!

[Fade to black, then for a split second, flash on a Riviera sunrise. Then back to black, and a voice over.]

Narrator: Time for a commercial break, *mesdames et messieurs*. The game that's on everyone's Christmas list this year. Have you been naughty or have you been nice? Time to play Domestic Wars!

[Fade up on a series of domestic encounters. First is set in Lydia's Paris flat, not quite a year after her wedding. She sits, resigned, at a table as her husband prepares to walk out. We can only see him from the back. He speaks with a heavy French accent.]

Husband: Whatever you think you want, Lydia, I can't give you. *Peut être* you'd be happier with one of your Siberian peasant blokes. I saw you flirting with... what's 'is name? Better figure it out before you're left in the gutter with your knickers down.

Narrator: Domestic Wars, on sale now!

[Cut to Amélie reclining on a sunlit terrace on the Riviera, overlooking a grove of palms. Underneath one of the trees is the American art critic Walter Pach, formerly a champion of Matisse.]

Pach: They're calling it obscene, Madame... Blue Nude... I blush.

Amélie: Oh, boo-hoo, poor you!

Pach: Those black outlines, the colours on the... they say it's you. You're the model.

Amelie: And if I am... it's just a painting.

Pach: I'm not sure... I mean, my review for the... you understand...

Amélie: Oh, *va foutre le camp,* Walter. You don't know me at all... I'm in my element when the house is burning. What does he say, that Wellington duke... publish and be damned!

Narrator: Domestic Wars, get yours today!

[Cut to a widow open onto a view of trees. A man wearing blue and white striped pajamas stands to the left of the window; a woman in a black dress sits to the right.]

Henri: You are ruining my life, Madame!

Amélie: Go! Go to hell... see how well you'll manage on your own!

Narrator: Domestic Wars, you know you want one!

[Cut to a photograph of Henri, Amelie, and Marguerite on a visit with friends, all seated round a table. At the far left is the young Olga Meerson, wannabe painter.]

Amélie: You think I don't see the way she moons around, Olga, yes Olga! Staring at you... like a calf in heat.

Henri: Don't be so silly, Melo... she wants to improve her painting, her technique.

Amélie: Her technique in the sack, you mean. Just don't embarrass yourself in front of Marguerite.

Henri: Please, Melo, don't go gaga on me. She's agreed to sit for me in exchange for lessons. *C'est tout!*

Narrator: Domestic Wars, next in the series!

[Another photograph. Amélie and Henri seated next to each other at a table in their apartment. Visible ageing on both their faces. A pet basket in on the floor, with a sleeping animal curled around itself.]

Amélie: You don't listen. You never listen. You don't even want to listen. You listen to her... Lydia... the foreigner... oh yes, for hours on end.

Henri: Let's not fight, *cherie*. She's a child. I know she looks like an ice princess, but she's a caring soul. Hasn't she been a good companion to you? Taking away the burden of the household? A trained nurse. For me as well. Yes, she's one of the best models as well. She and Marguerite.

Amélie: [she's rambling now, and suffering spinal pain] You just don't need me anymore. You used to need me. Now I'm useless... too fat to pose, too old to fuck. Marguerite and Georges had a baby boy. Do you even care? They're calling him Claude. We should find Camille and tell her. Why are you always so rude to Georges? Our daughter loves him... yet ever since she's become Madame Duthuit you've even changed toward her. Don't make her choose, Henri. Between a father and a husband you will never win!

Henri: Are those oranges still edible?

Amélie: Who's that in the basket down there... a puppy or a baby?

Henri [laughing]: Ah, Melo, you could always make me laugh. [To the dog.] Wakey, wakey, Raudi, is it time for your walk? Where are my little kitties? Where are they, Raudi? Minouche and Coussi? Let's go find them. Here kitty, kitty...

Amélie: I'm serious, Henri. You'd better find someone else. It's either her or me.

[Cut to a hospital ward, close on Marguerite's bed, her eyes closed, her upper body wrapped in bandages. Voices seep in from the past.]

She's been shot.

Who... Madame?

No, Mam'selle. The model, not the daughter.

What.... What are you talking about?

Shot, in the chest.

That's absurd!

Is she dead?

In the hospital. Touch and go.

Who'd want to shoot her?

She did it herself.

What are you talking about?

[Three ward doctors examine Lydia, comparing notes.]

Doctor 1: She must be made in a factory... how can she survive such a direct shot?

Doctor 2: In fact, what do we know about her, if anything. Is she married? Next of kin?

Doctor 3: [flipping through medical records] There was a husband, Omeltchenko... Siberian chappie, looks like they split up. First marriage to a Frenchman, also split.

Doctor 1: Maybe she's a gold digger.

Doctor 3: Says here she's a trained nurse.

Doctor 2: So what's she doing working as a film extra, dancing in cafes, waiting on tables? Hmm, last known employment with the Matisse family.

Doctor 1: Uh oh, that means trouble!

Doctor 3: Madame kicked her out. Apparently.

Doctor 2: Well, we can still send them the bill. Last known address.

Doctor 3: Let's keep her under observation before we discharge her.

Doctor 1: Constitution of an elephant!

[Once again the screen fills with a patchwork of tiny images, one prominently lit up. This time the interview is with Sergei Shchukin, one of the most important art collectors of the era. He wears a Panama-style hat and lightweight three-piece suit, the jacket unbuttoned. A tipped walking stick rests across his lap. His short beard in neatly trimmed. His expression inviting conversation.]

Auteur: Comrade Shchukin, *spasiba* for this interview... it is a great honour to meet you.

Sergei: Please call me Sergei. We are on the same side, yes? Spreading the gospel of Saint Henri!

Auteur: And yet you called him a madman. Is that what you really thought?

Sergei: Of course not. It was a joke to poke in the eye of those philistines in Paris and Moscow. They couldn't understand why I'd bought so many of his canvases. I told them, "A madman painted it and a madman bought it."

Auteur: But you kept all your collection private... not for show to the public. Why?

Sergei: Only at first. You are correct, though. I think it is in the nature of the collector... to own, to possess. Something physical, not ephemeral, like love or friendship. The statue is mine, I can touch it. The painting will not disappear in the dawn.

Auteur: I don't want to raise old wounds, Sergei, but do you make any connection between the challenge to collect art...

Sergei: ... a challenge I truly believe was set to me by God...

Auteur: ... uhm, yes, and the tragic death of your young son by his own hand. Followed into the grave by your wife Lidya and then your brother Ivan. Please forgive me if ...

Sergei: Who knows why we do what we do. I sought solace in the desert, like Saint Simon. Only God has the answers. Are you a believer, Mam'selle?

Auteur: Perhaps not in the way you...

Sergei: Matisse intrigued me. It was a wholly new approach. He never stopped. He couldn't help himself. It didn't matter whether he was poor or had a kopek. So I commissioned several large canvasses and studies for each. Women holding hands dancing in a circle. Simple. Yet a window on the soul of the world. I daresay the money came in handy.

Auteur: How did you decide which paintings you wanted. He was churning them... like a madman.

Sergei: Well, did you know I locked myself away, this is the truth, Mam'selle... and I have a magnificent home in Moscow... I was under strict orders not to be disturbed. And every day and every night I tried the paintings on my eyes. As if they were a suit of clothes. For weeks. Until I knew. This one. And this. And that as well. And I was never wrong, and never once did I have any regrets.

Auteur: And you invited him to Moscow, when was that? 1911? How had you heard about his work in the first place?

Sergei: There were two of us, myself and Ivan, both grown rich as clothiers, popping up in Paris and Moscow. Not rivals exactly, but interested in the same sort of thing. Forcing the buyers with francs and roubles to look up from their Giottos and Constables. I'd already had deep discussions with Gauguin. I loved Monet and Cézanne and Dutch Vincent. Now he really was a madman, but the paint, the colours... he was obsessed. These new guys released the wild beasts from their cages. And Henri was running along with them. So I brought him to Moscow to see what we could see.

Auteur: Is that when he discovered wooden icons? He wrote about them as though they were the Holy Grail. Painted with simplicity, he said.

Sergei: Yes, that's exactly how he felt. He was exhausted by the trip, but every day he went to see the icons at the Tretyakov Gallery. And even more at nearby churches, and convents. He called them great art. He said, "Just to see them, we ought to learn how to understand art."

[Suddenly one of the tiny images in the background begins fla shing, accompanied by the sounds of a siren. Matisse himself takes over the screen.]

Henri: That's enough, *mes amis*. Please stop this, right now.

Sergei: Calm down, Henri.

Henri: *Non, non*! Mam'selle, this will only lead to tears. Sergei's story turns so far in on itself... you need a different film, one about him. Meanwhile, I'm getting older by the minute. We just don't have the time.

Auteur: Has he said anything untrue?

Henri: That's not the point. Yes, Sergei, you saved me with your commission for The Dance, you really did. But we can't go into battle with the Tsar, the Bolsheviks, and the Communists or we'll be here all night. And, frankly, I really don't trust you. You're in the aura of this one, this Stein person. [He turns to the screen of images, and pushes at one, which grows to full size. It's Gertrude Stein.]

Yes, speaking of trust, you can just get the hell out of here, you fat dyke, I have a bone to pick. So shut up and listen. Why have you been spreading garbage about my Amélie? You always think you know everything. You think because you and your brother Leo bought some of my paintings, that you invited us to stay at your villa in Fiesole, that gives you the right to badmouth my wife.

She's beautiful, kind and strong. You're vindictive and ugly. I can forgive you the latter, there is beauty in everything... but never the former. Never! I suspect you merely wanted to gather information to throw back at her later. That's what you do, isn't it? Spread gloom with your silly little verses and meetings with the Vichy traitors. You are phony baloney, Gertrude.

Stirring it up, always stirring it up... like the lies about me and Picasso. He's got more talent in his hangnail than you have in all your avoirdupois. We're great friends, Pablo and I, so stop putting it about we're enemies. The only enemy I have here is you, Madame. At least your brother Michael and his wife are civil. And on the right side of this fucking war.

[Now we can hear other over-lapping voices from the divisions onscreen. Some louder than others. Two dominate. They are the Cone sisters, also important collectors of Matisse. As well as of Picasso. They speak as one, as in life, often finishing each other's sentences. They speak in the Baltimore accents of their birth.]

The Cones: What about us? We paid him good money. We helped when others mocked. We assured the American public knew about him.

{But their voices are fading as the scene cuts to black. In the distance, and getting louder, we can hear the squeaking of tiny mice. Very slowly the screen fills with blocks of primary colours – the brightest red, deep royal blue, and sunshine yellow. Over the sound of the mice we hear the voice of the Narrator.]

Narrator: *Mesdames et Messieurs*. We cannot today present to you Mortimer Mouse as Steamboat Willie. Nor that other rodent, Mickey, so beloved of children around the world. Yes, they were the first cartoon mice, but M'sieur Uncle Walt is a litigious animator, so let's continue Henri's story with these sweet little white lab mice.

[In one corner of the screen, the mice present an easel on which is a large pad of drawing paper, the kind used for lectures. One mouse carries another on its little shoulders; it holds a long pointer, tapping at each new item of the following narration. During this, the other mice confer, repeating the points in the high-pitched tones of cartoon animals.]

It is a truth universally acknowledged that a single man in possession of good fortune must be in want of a home. Preferably with a studio attached. Where he can play his violin at all hours of the day and night. And where he might keep a flock of pigeons and doves loose in one of the rooms, along with a doggie and perhaps some cats. And whether he has a fortune or not. But who may be plagued with the demon desire to paint and sculpt and draw at all costs, whether to his family life or his fragile health. Or both.

Which is why Henri moved around with the frequency of the changing scenes in a cartoon. Help me out here, little mice. Show the nice ladies and gentlemen pictures of his homes. [The mice chirp, gather together, pushing images of the various residences into frame as the narration continues.] Big slabs of colour backing up his apartments, hotel rooms, little houses, big studios, Paris, Nice, New York, Moscow.

The mice scamper this way and that in all directions, sometimes pausing briefly for some explanatory remarks. The images include

- Le Cateau-Cambrésis in Picardy, rue du Chene Arnaud where he was born
- Bohain-en-Vermandois, 24 rue Fagard where he grew up
- Saint-Quentin where he was a young lawyer
- 1891/2 fifth-floor Paris apartment at 19 quai Saint-Michel with Camille Joblaud for his first formal painting lessons
- 1898 Amélie, now Madame Matisse, moved with him to another apartment in the same building, also on the fifth floor, but with more windows.
- Belle Isle, Brittany to which he and Amélie returned a few times
- rue de Châteaudun just down the street from Amélie's hat shop
- London
- Corsica
- 1900 World's Fair, Paris
- Much travel by ship and rail
- Catalan port of Collioure, in the south of France, where Henri loved the views

- 1905 Henri stayed in Nice, while Amélie continued in Paris to complete the course of injections on her spine. One of his pleasures was walking the family dog Ghika.
- From 1906 -1917 Henri lived in Paris and established his home, studio, and school at Hôtel Biron
- In 1907 the couple were well enough for a trip to Venice and Padua. In Florence they were guests of the Steins in their villa in Fiesole. They used it as a base to explore the early Italian classics such as Piero della Francesca and the Sienna school.
- In 1909 the Matisse family lived in a former convent on the Boulevard des Invalides, in Paris, where the artist conducted his own painting school, the Académie Matisse.
- At the time they took advantage of Shchukin's generosity, which provided them with a comfortable house in Issy-les-Moulineaux. It was a remarkable gesture for a patron, though the couple continued to be plagued by health issues. For much of the time Henri had to leave his wife at home while he spent months away in Tahiti, Morocco, and New York.
- After a period of relative good health, they felt well enough to travel. In 1934 they rented Villa Lou Mandiou near St Jean-Cap Ferrat harbour for two months.

[Suddenly the parade of venues buffers to a standstill. A remote control tape recording continues the narrative, while the group of mice confer in a corner of the screen, framed against panels of primary colours.]

Tape Machine: Although their marriage was still somewhat fragile, the Matisses had decided to stay on in Nice when their lease expired at Place Charles-Félix in the summer of 1938. To this end they had already bought two adjacent apartments in January that same year on the third floor in the old Excelsior-Regina Palace, the last and grandest of Nice's imperial hotels, located above Nice in the hills of Cimiez. During renovation work on their new apartments, Matisse stayed at the British Hotel during the months of September and October and then moved into his new home in mid-November.

Henri's voice: Hey, mice! What's the deal? What are you guys doing?

[The mice break, each holding signs reading "on strike." One larger sign says "Too much running around."]

Henri: On strike? You're mice, *nom de Dieu*... and cartoon mice at that. What have you got to strike about? [The mice squeak in a higher pitch, very difficult to decipher, though Henri manages.] Demands? What demands? Don't forget, I'm a trained lawyer. [One mouse comes forward as a spokes-mouse. Henri repeats after him.] Better quality of grain... agreed. Gargles and throat lozenges offscreen to save our voices. Sounds reasonable. Agreed. Taking jobs away from human actors? But... wait... doesn't that mean you're voting to lose work? Yes, all right, I agree it's exploitation. Anything else? You want to star in the next movie?! Why, you little rats... I mean mice. [Henri chases them to the bottom of the screen. His voice now directly copies Porky Pig's lisp at the end of the Loony Toons cartoons; the mice are enclosed in a brightly coloured carton circle, which fades to a black screen accompanied by the closing theme music.] Th-th-th-that's all folks!

[Fade to black. Slow fade up to an extreme close-up on Henri's troubled face. As the shot widens, we see he's in a hospital bed. This is the final, extended sequence. It takes in the past, present, and future and relies on a stream-of-consciousness within Henri's fevered brain as he faces the dangers of a life-or-death operation. It will leave him having to use a colostomy bag for the remainder of his life. Which will be about ten years. Most of the sequence finds him alone, but occasionally he has brief visits – real or imagined - from Amélie, the doctors, Marguerite, Picasso, and especially Lydia.

Henri, covered in sweat is near delirium. We hear tango music, faint at first, then louder and louder. Henri watches himself whirling around his bed, dressed in a full-length dressing gown and jaunty black silk nightcap. The number is '*Poule de Luxe*.' Amélie's voice breaks across the music. She's excited, laughing.]

Amélie: You're dancing, my love. They won't know anything like it in New York. *Poule de Luxe*... a prostitute... they won't know what hit them. A dance called a hooker, isn't that what they call it?

Henri: But you didn't come with me, Amélie. You didn't come along. I booked a double cabin to Tahiti. I had to dance alone.

Amélie: Too painful, *cheri*. I couldn't move.

Henri: How will you manage? Marguerite needs her operation. Throat cancer. Our little girl.

Amélie: It's all right. My sister's coming. Berthe will look after me.

Henri: Where am I? Is this the hospital in Nice? They said it's an ulcer. Who are you? [A Dominican nun in full nursing habit takes Henri's pulse and checks his temperature with an oral thermometer. He tries to speak, but the nun just shakes her head. But as soon as she removes the thermometer, he asks again:] Who are you? Where am I?

Nun: The doctors will be along shortly. You're at the Parc de Lyon Clinic. Try to get some rest.

Henri: Lydia! Where are you, Amélie's in pain. You have the touch. Who's looking after the birds. They need special ants to eat. Who's cleaning up the poop. How many are there, now cherie? Hundreds... more! Pigeons. Parakeets. The cats are very good, very well behaved. When the birds sing, they sit and wait. Minouche and Coussi, my little fluffies.

Lydia: You are so funny, Henri. Sitting there with a bird on your head. We had to dismiss the bird man. Remember? It was the war. Couldn't get the supplies.

Picasso: Henri, *Querido amigo, ¿Cómo te va?*... I like your hat... oh, wait, listen... your hat is singing.

Henri: Pablo, you whippersnapper! We are brothers, *n'est-ce pas*? You have pigeons. I have pigeons. And doves. We can swap. Here, look, this one is special.

Picasso: She's a beauty! I know just where to put her.

Henri: Not in the oven, comrade.

Doctor Santy: And how are we today, Monsieur? Fever's down, I see. [He consults with his assistant surgeon Dr Leriche.]

Henri: What have you done to me, Docteur? Why is my stomach on fire?

Lydia: You've had your colon removed, Henri. You know that, you agreed. These doctors saved your life.

Henri: I'm dying. How can I paint without a colon. Nowhere to put the brushes.

Lydia: Is this what you're going to be like when we get home. Are you going to keep me on the run?

Henri: I suppose you'll have to plonk me in a wheelchair. I can't walk, can I? And what about the shit-bag, will you take care of that as well?

Lydia: Yes, Henri, I will. I told you. I can pose when you're ready, and if not, you won't have to worry about anything. I have the scissors all ready for the cut-outs. The studio is bright and clean. The patterns and sketches are set out in order. The blue nudes will set fire to the eyes of the world.

Henri: I can't believe you were working as a movie extra when I found you. Who could write a script like that?! I know you like the back of my hand, just from the way the light lights up your body. You're like one of my own children. I loved painting you all. Now I can't.

Lydia: We'll manage, old man.

Henri: You came back, Lydia. She said to choose, and then she left. But you came back. Where did you go?

[We hear platform announcements from the main meeting point of the Gare St. Lazare. Amélie sits on the bed, dressed for travel. She hands him the final divorce papers as she chatters away, her words unheard by us. Instead we hear Henri's thoughts, quoting to the doctor from a letter he was to write afterward.]

Henri: Did I tell you, Docteur... My wife never looked at me, there in the station, but I didn't take my eyes off her. I couldn't get a word out. I stood as still as if I were a statue of wood. I swore never to be caught that way again. I'm going to try to isolate myself as if I were still absent. Is that a good plan, in your professional opinion. [He looks around the room, searching for something, or someone.] Marguerite, my Margot-Largo... sing to me. Your lovely voice. Where are you, little one?

[Marguerite tries to answer but her throat is blocked by a tube that trails from her lips. She's undergone a tracheotomy and will never sing again. But she speaks to him from the future. Bringing devastating news.]

Marguerite's croaky voice: It's April, Papa, 1944. The Gestapo got me in Rennes. Maman aussi, in Paris. Punishment, hard labour... just for delivering leaflets for the Resistance. But the Allies are coming to the coast. Guaranteed. Maman will be free in August, and I will be, too, by October.

Henri: For fuck's sake... is there any illness or disaster in this world that has left Matisse alone?

[After a beat, Picasso sticks his head through the curtain around Henri's bed, like a Commedia dell'arte clown.]

Picasso: If she is not a dove of war, then what is she, eh Henri?

[And they speak in unison.]

Henri and Picasso: The Dove of Peace.

[Cut to Picasso's iconic dove on the wing and landing on the final image of the painting Woman in a Purple Coat, a painting from 1937 of Lydia. Super-imposed is the caption: December 1869 – November 1954. We hear Henri's voice-over.]

Henri: That will do.

***

KWICKIE KAPTION 4

Sandro Botticelli's late 15th century masterpiece *Nascita di Venere* [the Birth of Venus] depicts the goddess washing up on shore and fully-grown. It's displayed in the Uffizi Gallery in Florence.

Are you sure this is how I get to be a Page Three girl?

CHAPTER SEVEN – ALADDIN'S CAVE

Up Housewives And At 'Em! Yates Wilson 1939/40

London's Imperial War Museum contains an important collection of World War Two posters especially commissioned by the War Office. From the beginning of the so-called Phony War right through to imparting advice both to service men and those on the home front, British artists brought their original styles to eye-catching messages. Standing out from the more sober, text-based examples are the witty [Loose Lips Sink Ships], or cajoling [We Want Your Kitchen Waste], and eventually some finger-wagging admonitory [Don't Waste Oil]. The ever-popular cartoonist Giles provided a few political illustrations at the time.

As the war stumbled on, the ubiquitous posters and magazine reproductions reflected changing social values, perhaps the most salient being women filling in for volunteers and military recruits. Land girls, factory workers, and the draft of female auxiliaries in the forces were depicted as well as championing the role of housewives. The main task was to boost morale and assure solid support for the war effort, especially in the face of fake news and doom-laden propaganda by the enemy.

The poster known as *Up Housewives And At 'Em!* issued early in the war, entreats women to collect material that can be recycled for military use. The credited illustrator is Yates Wilson, but there's almost nothing in the public domain about him. His bold and colourful style is recognisable on a few other sites, including the archives of *John Bull* magazine, whose December 1947 front cover reproduces a scene in the Arsenal dressing room. Wilson signed *The Christening*, quite reminiscent of Norman Rockwell; it depicts a proud young sailor carrying his new baby, flanked by his wife and possibly the granny, and features on a website called Artnet. Another site, the Advertising Archives, celebrates the 'new man,' with Wilson's post-war hero clad in a pink pinny, puffing on a pipe, and sporting a golden halo as he washes the dishes.

His work pops up in 1959 in an unexpected context as the author and illustrator of the follow-on adventures of Lewis Carroll's most famous girl. The book is called *More Alice*.

My own story begins with the three women on the poster, following their determined efforts to keep some kind of balance as the war threatens to tip them into real danger. The discovery of betrayal in their midst pierces them all as sharply as gunfire.

Even the early days were punctuated by strict blackout orders, allowing no escaped light to provide Luftwaffe targets throughout the country. It wasn't until November 1939 that the German planes finally released their destructive cargo. I hope the series of brief scenes, as though emerging from blackouts, reproduces the sense of disconnect and anxiety affecting folk in all walks of life.

Aladdin's Cave

As usual, Myrtle's lardy cake cooled on the serving plate in anticipation. Their favourite. The tea steeped in the big family pot inherited from her own mother, and she'd saved some condensed milk from her rations. On those rare occasions in the past with all the family around the table, the capacious Brown Betty teapot with its shiny Rockingham glaze had served everyone at least one cuppa. Even with just the three of them today, Myrtle took comfort in its familiarity, hoping her girls would as well.

A sunny day, not warm enough to still count as summer, however much the townsfolk held onto the memory. The house stood proud at the end of the High Street, bounded by the Common. Cricket. Children giving chase. Doggies running, sniffing, fetching for approval and a kind word. The grass vibrant, and the trees hanging onto their leaves for dear life.

1940 had already passed its half-way mark, but from the time she first moved in over thirty years ago, Myrtle never tired of the view from the big kitchen window. Swags of flowered chintz and stripes, panes polished to invisibility. Such a dutiful housewife. Everyone said so. Taking the trouble.

Trouble had been sneaking around lately, everyone suspected, what with all the rumours. Like so many, Myrtle tried to look another way, kept herself busy, busy, buzzy as a busy bee. She relished this time out, so precious, with Rose, her eldest and the baby Jasmine. Some baby! A handful, more like! She'd recently celebrated her seventeenth, and Myrtle wondered, like so many mothers, where all the time had gone. Jaz would always be her baby, no matter how old, and no matter what stories she brought home from the dances at the church hall in the next village. That new beau she called Lance sounded like quite a card! "Mum," helping herself to another slice of cake, "did I tell you...?"

Rose had heard it all before.

BLACKOUT

The townsfolk didn't call this one The Great War. They barely called it anything. "Over by Christmas," said many, swiping away the foam from their pints down the pub. Echoing the very phrase they'd used, or heard their parents use at the start of that other war. The Great One.

But ask anyone who's done the actual fighting – invalided out with shrapnel wounds and shell-shock, or eye-witness to the cannon blasts that turned mud red in the trenches – ask anyone, and they won't call their war Great. They'll call it a waste of human life, even if they accept a medal for their trouble. Lest we forget.

Everyone listened to the wireless, armchair generals all. "Over by Christmas." Fathers pulling on the tobacco in their pipes said, "It's official, Mother. You heard it on the wireless, so don't worry your head over the rumours. Let us men do our jobs."

BLACKOUT

Felix entered the breakfast room to join his wife and son. They were still in pajamas, hers silk, the boy's cosy flannel, but Felix was dressed for business. He made his excuses: "Sorry, urgent telephone call. I could murder a strong coffee." But as he bent to kiss her, she stood and, with great excitement, whispered in his ear.

He embraced his wife with genuine warmth. "Are you sure, my darling?" She was happy to confirm, the tears on her cheeks of joy. Bound together as much by affection as finance, it was, if not quite a marriage of true minds, then surely one of equal genealogical traceability. Approving heads at their nuptials some years before nodded under big-brimmed hats, fluffy feathers waving like fledglings. Rooted in the stuffy rooms of their ancestors, they both wanted to break through to a place of freedom, to the joy of youth. No one, whatever their net worth, stops time.

And no one wants a repeat of the infernal wailing after last year's false alarm. A nursery, months of choosing wallpapers, little cupboards, a cradle. Empty. Unused. Not her husband nor her tight-lipped mother could soothe those tears. "Honora," her mother tried to combine maternal concern with a sort of disapproval. "In your stride, dear, in your stride." Oh, yes, even the rich do laugh and cry.

This time, though, she was sure, and she knew that Felix would attend to every minute detail for the months of her confinement. Little Orlando was nearly five; they agreed another child would complete the family.

"Mummy, eated all my eggy."

"What a good boy, Lando. Up to your room and play, now." She stood to watch him go, and Felix joined her. He rang the little bell on the sideboard. Someone would clear away the plates. They were so happy, and time stopped as they grinned at each other.

"Baby should pop before Christmas." She snuggled into the lightweight wool of his jacket. The grey one she'd helped him choose. He pulled her at arms' length to see her face. An announcement. He tried to imitate the tone of his mother-in-law.

"Honora!"

Giggling. "Well, that sounds serious."

"No, really, Onnie... let's go up to town. Celebrate! Supper at Simpsons. Suite at the Savoy."

"What a jolly idea!" she said.

"Before you get too broad to fit through the door," he teased, giving her bottom a friendly slap.

"You are a truly terrible man, Sir Felix Humble." It didn't escape her notice it was exactly how he dismissed his dappled mare. She traced his clipped moustache with her forefinger, loving the way it completely matched his eyebrows. Colour. Curve. A complete set.

He took time for the tingle at the back of his neck when she touched him, and, after a slight pause, asked, "Where's Nanny Slater?" She might have wagged a finger at such an administrative oversight, but merely reminded him they'd given her permission to stay with her elderly mother. "On her last legs, apparently. Near Oxford."

He kissed her. "Whatever would I do without you, my love?"

Was that a hint of triumph in her smile? "I'll get that girl, what's-her-name, Myrtle's daughter, to look after Lando. He likes her."

BLACKOUT

Just months before they had called it the Phony War because those rumours - of conflict, of invasion, of the enemy floating down from the sky and slitting throats in the middle of the night - those rumours were proving to be unfounded. So far. So far, so good. No fighting reported on the wireless. Plenty of meetings though, men in black suits sitting around tables, plenty of talking. No fighting either in those Pathé newsreels they showed at the cinema, or in the daily paper headlines.

But those who were making real decisions, those black-suited men, acting on real knowledge, were preparing the people for more fighting than the whole world had ever known. And then the sorties started. Tentative. A taster of terror. London. Scotland. The Channel coast. Plenty more to come. But when? You had to be in the know. With his close contacts in Parliament and on the Exchange, Sir Felix knew quite a bit.

People hesitated to look across the horizon of reality as though at a board game. Children repeated words they couldn't understand, and pretended broom handles were rifles. Bang-bang. You're dead! Shouting – AAarrrgghh! - before they clutched their shoulders in mock agony and fell down, plop! Like the bad guys in the films. Pastimes and games.

Every city, town, and village was prepared. ARP Wardens fastened the chin straps on their steel helmets and sallied forth to enforce blackouts. The Air Raid Precautions units had been set up by the government, and the wardens, loyal subjects to a man, wanted to do their bit when age or some infirmity prevented enlisting.

They donated their front rooms or High Street shops as ARP HQ, and wore the big yellow 'W' on their patrol helmets with pride. They could demand, without fear nor favour, "Douse those lights,

Missus," and "Pull those curtains to." Everyone had been pre-warned to wait for the all clear. A sound once heard, never forgot.

Nought to fear but fear itself. Well, not much anyroad.

BLACKOUT

The Flower Girls. Everyone called them The Flower Girls. Myrtle, Rose, and Jasmine. Mum, two daughters. There had been sons as well, of course, but Myrtle knew what people called her and the girls. Bound together in one delicate bouquet, spreading the scent of an era, sweet fragrance. But left too long, like Shakespeare's lilies, they make you puke. Contradiction: the beating heart of this story.

Such is the progress of global disaster, and woe betide those who get trapped under its rubble.

MYRTLE

There must have been a time, surely, a childhood of smiles and softness, but now, in her fiftieth year, anyone who knew Myrtle described her as 'no nonsense.' That set jaw of determination, whatever the task, was her way of coping. Her life hadn't always been steady as sunrise, but she didn't dwell. Well, only a bit. Today, for example. Waiting for the girls to arrive for their fortnightly trip to the Primary School collection point. Rose would bring Macavity, her Scottie, such a sweet-tempered thing. "Fancy naming a dog after a cat!" she'd said. "Everyone's reading Mr Eliot's book, Mum." And they'd all walk down the High Street with their bags of papers and bones. Doing their bit for king and country.

Those moments of waiting tempted deeper memories. The images jumbled up together, no mental accounts ledger. There, on the sideboard, a sepia wedding photo of her and Seth beckoned her back. Married at eighteen, though he was much older, a widower. Earned a good living on contract as farrier to the local brewery. Called in from time to time to tend the stable horses at the county's stately homes. Sampled the hoppy ale of a Saturday night, but he'd roll home singing, never fighting. And up early for Matins next day. A God-fearing man, a rock.

That was before the church was blitzed in a German air attack... Myrtle would never forget that sound, hiding under the kitchen table, fingers in her ears to block the noise. Before the fireballs came a note, some crazy music made by locusts, louder and louder still; then a sort of whoosh, and finally boom-booming, like rifles competing on a duck shoot.

A sermon a week, said Seth, and his wife by his side. Myrtle made sure his good suit was pressed and her bonnet none too fancy. They were calling it the Jazz Age across the pond, but Home Counties market towns like theirs were still catching up with last century's fashions. She'd seen the glossy magazines that Jasmine brought home.

As the family grew Seth shepherded all the little ones into the building he always called The House of God. His pride could hardly be thought one of the Gospel's catalogued sins; it was more a celebration of life after his previous marriage of barren disappointment. The children were living proof it wasn't his fault.

Never instructed in the expectations of her nuptial duties, Myrtle accepted that her role was to breed. Now, waiting for her girls, she allowed herself a litany:

They tried all right, following Seth's nightly urgings, but she didn't conceive for the first months. Then in 1908, she delivered a premature son who died at birth. Tiny thing, she only caught a blurred glimpse when the midwife whisked him away. They didn't name those babies back then, shaming mothers into unspoken failure, and no time to grieve with so many chores. Was it then Seth made friends down the pub? Or did that come later? She couldn't remember. Close your eyes and think of England, the advice every girl was given. Their idea of sex education.

After a couple of years, Rose arrived, strong, healthy and screaming her lungs out. Seth knocked on the door to see what all the fuss was about. "Get out!" the midwife ordered. He retreated to his pub pals, handing out cigars, puffing out his chest as though it was he who'd given birth. So Myrtle had later been told.

He was even prouder when Reggie was born. Well, every father wants a boy. His son. Reginald John. Healthy, to be sure, but not an easy child. Always getting into scrapes and quick to rile. Neither Seth nor Myrtle knew why he was so eager to fight. As he got older, they thought he'd settle after he 'knocked up that Irish wench' [as Seth told it], and had to be marched to the altar. Her brothers toted rifles and growled. Both his new wife and the baby died on Myrtle's dining table in the front room. Reggie screamed a rainbow of anger, blaming his father, blaming 'that slut and her gangster brothers,' blaming everyone he could before he took off.

He couldn't run away fast enough, nor far enough, and joined the Merchant Navy. Broke Myrtle's heart. Sometimes he'd send a post card of brief clichés, but they were few and far between. Strange squiggly writing across the stamps. She'd kept them all, tied together with grosgrain ribbon, tucked into a cigar box. It was decorated with a picture of a horse. Sometimes she took the wooden box down from the top of her wardrobe. Nowadays she needed her glasses to read the words, but she could still smell the cedar, though it faded with every year.

Of Myrtle's next two pregnancies, one was cut short in a miscarriage, and the next at age 28 resolved with a baby delivered before term, stillborn, blue, unmoving. Seth needed more to prove his potency, and a year later, barely time for his wife to recover, their son Matthew was born. Not as sporty as his father would have liked, but all requisite parts intact. A placid child, no trouble at all. Fussed over from the first, he baffled them, his family.

Baby Matty didn't speak a word till he was two, and then you couldn't shut him up. So many questions, wanting to know everything. He could read before the age of three, and filled any empty bits of paper with astounding drawings of his parents and neighbours. Seth felt a sense of triumph when the little boy smiled; he adored being thrown into the air and caught in his father's bear hug. But he struggled to find the right words for a conversation... the boy showed no interest in horses or their care.

They called him Matt, and Rosie teased him as Door-Matt. He excelled at his studies and was encouraged by the teachers and priests to take up a training place studying Art & Design, which had newly been added to the curriculum. He had no urgent ambition; the prospect of teaching in the local school suited him. He was happiest closest to home. Myrtle never quite understood him, but he was treasured as an exciting gift. Her best boy.

But, as many mothers know, it's the baby of the family who spoons up the spoils of love. As a toddler Jaz was plump, tasting everything from the biscuits in the puppy's bowl to Seth's teeth whitener, exploring corners and pockets, raiding Myrtle's cupboard to play dress-up. As she slimmed down into a feisty youngster, the whole family couldn't help but adore her. She was everyone's baby.

It all changed on the 'baby's' fifth birthday. Myrtle had invited Jazzie's playmates to the house for cake and board games. Seth was under orders to bring a crock of honey from the brewery's store so she could sweeten her homemade lemonade for the children. But as he was about to set off, he was called back to the stables. One of the dray horses was limping badly, eyes wild with pain. Seth diagnosed awns of grain under the hoof. He pushed the jug of honey down into his pocket, took out the hook-ended hoof knife and set to work. He warned the stable boy to hold tight the reins, but they slipped from his grasp. The horse lashed out with both hind legs, kicking such a blow to Seth's head he was unconscious for days. The honey crock shattered and golden liquid seeped from the horse's stall coating the stable floor.

Someone at the brewery arranged the ambulance; picked up the tab. They haggled over the cost of the hospital, but farriers with Seth's expertise were few and far between. Somehow, Myrtle managed, and the children filled the birthday party with shrieks of laughter. They left with tummies full of sugar and polite handshakes. Jasmine was drawn to the stack of presents on the sideboard, and the unshakeable certainty that whatever had happened to her father was her fault.

Myrtle had rejoiced with her eldest when Arthur proposed the previous year. He ran the Ironmongers on the High Street and was considered a good catch, despite being a widower with two youngsters to raise. Rose was certainly smitten, she could see that. They'd wanted to marry straight away, but Myrtle wore herself out nursing Seth at home, and her general decline in spirit gave Rose pause. It was obvious to all her mother was falling deeper into a blue funk. She knew her filial duty. Arthur had no choice; he could only agree to wait.

Nothing was the same after the accident. Seth resented that he could only walk with a cane, and his speech slurred like a drunkard. He hated the inability to control his words, finding refuge in the pub, his second home. Drowning his rage. When he did reel up the road, Rose heard him shouting foul curses. From her bedroom she cringed at the sound of his hit and miss blows that left her mother bruised, in pain. Terrified by the noise, little Jazzie appeared in her sister's doorway. Rose threw back the blanket and cuddled her through the night.

But Myrtle refused to take any action against him. "He'll sleep it off," was her stock reply. Then, just like that, from one day to the next, he was dead. It may sound cruel, and so the townsfolk whispered, but it was for the best.

ROSE

Rose knew all about the ARP; she not only gave her full support to the protection they provided her family, she felt as responsible for their success as if she represented them in Westminster. Her husband Arthur was a warden, and proud of it. There hadn't been any great rush for the men of the town to enlist, but even if he could, not only did he have a family to support, the cataract clouding his left eye meant rejection. Rose helped set up his ARP base at the back of their Ironmongers on the High Street, cleared a space for meetings, and the shelving for their masks and equipment. She and Arthur agreed to apprentice his son John in the shop, his sharp vision a great help to his father.

At fifteen, daughter Hazel was about to leave school, and concentrating on having fun with Rose's baby sister. The future declared itself before her, like a billboard promising adventure in bold, bright colours. They called her Haze, but her mind was water-clear. She and her older brother were burdened with a terrible task. The death of their mother from influenza not only left them unable to comprehend the power of disease, but they felt responsible for their father's grief. They could comfort each other, but had no tricks or tools to bring Arthur's smile back.

They coped in different ways: John determined in his self-appointed role as deputy to his father; Hazel abandoning all the acceptable stages from childhood to maturity, excavating her own road. 'Crazy Hazey, daft as Maisie,' her school mates teased; though no one knew who Maisie was. When Rose came into their lives, they both saw how happy she made Arthur. She knew not to attempt to replace their mother, but she earned their trust with her easy hugs and a complete welcome into her family. Their family.

Some claim women past thirty shouldn't have children, but she and Arthur rejoiced when she fell pregnant. Little Basil was their perfect baby, now a toddler of four. Before he was born, the whole family sipped cups of newly rationed tea, testing out names. It had become a family ritual, an amusing pastime. They all immediately agreed to Hazel's passionate suggestion to call the baby after her favourite film actor Basil Rathbone. "Oh, you know, Daddy... Robin Hood, Sherlock Holmes." Sounded like a touch of class to Rose. And now she was expecting another bundle of joy. A Christmas present that wouldn't need wrapping.

As for the close friendship between Hazel and Jasmine, Rose was convinced the two had swallowed the seeds of adventure and daring in the womb. Neither she nor Arthur begrudged them the chance to spread their wings. It was, after all, what they both yearned for themselves... if the damn war weren't blocking the very air they breathed. And beyond.

Arthur considered opening the Ironmongers one of the best decisions he'd ever made; his wife's support gave him the courage to continue every day. He'd started as a door-to-door merchant, offering bargains to housewives throughout the county. When he moved to the town, he'd already made contacts with the most reliable suppliers. Once he let Rose in on the running of the shop, they knew they could turn it into something special. By stocking so many everyday items that the townsfolk would always need, not only was their living assured, they became well known in the community. Always keen to share advice, help out where they could.

They supported local charities, and Rose was proud to be inducted into the Women's Institute, attending meetings when she could. She listened politely whenever Lady Honora rose to speak. "A bit young for a chair person," she confessed to her brother; he'd become quite a confidante. Matty repeated something he'd heard his friend Isabella say, "The privilege of position."

That was when they'd met up in London last spring to attend The Festival of Music, an avowedly left wing concert, including a pageant for hundreds of singers and dancers. Soviet folk songs and a selection of ballads from Mr Britten collaborating with Mr Auden. But Matt had been most impressed by the bass tones from Mr Robeson. "Rich as Mum's gravy. You could feel it inside your bones, Rosie," he'd said. And then, "I think I'm in love."

"With Mr Robeson?" she'd teased.

It was women especially who grew to depend on the Ironmongers, for gossip and deeper friendships, without the rigour of the church, and the unpredictability of the pub. True, the shop didn't offer activity like the Primary School Hall, but if a housewife wanted a key cut on that new-fangled machine, a fluffed-up feather duster, or a replacement for those leaky rubber gloves, just ask Arthur or John. If Rose happened to be in, she was sure to invite them for a cuppa and a home-baked biscuit. And when little Basil crept under the table to play with his toys, no one was ever offended when the cheeky monkey tugged at their skirts.

JASMINE

They'd both seen the advertisements for Gravy Legs and Liquid Stockings, but this was far less dear. Jasmine 'borrowed' her sister Rose's kohl stick. Lots of women were using them, and there were even tips on technique in that magazine column. Best was to get a pal to help. Bit of luck, then, that Jaz

had her niece Hazel. Well, niece by marriage.

"Hold still, Haze, Don't wanna smear the line."

They'd already gone through the tedious ritual. First bathe and exfoliate with a loofah. Hazel knew her father sold stiff natural sponge loofah's in the shop; she asked her brother John to get one. Jasmine also relied on her brother, Matt. He helped her find the definition of 'exfoliate,' in his two-volume dictionary. He also agreed to let them use his new safety razor.

Though never as ebullient as his sister, he was just as eager to discover images of the future. A future, he was now convinced, that would include Isabella. The last time she'd come home for the holidays from her studies at the Sorbonne, she'd let him put his arm around her at the cinema, and they held hands on the way home. He wasn't at all intimidated by her intelligence and quick wit; she'd run rings around him with the latest American slang learned from the G.I.s stationed in Paris. She may be surrounded by French ooo-la-la, he thought, but she was a county lass through and through. No nonsense. Like his Mum. "Izzy," he teased her, "you're a marvel on two legs!"

And she shot straight back with "Well, Matty dear, would you prefer me on four?"

The girls had smoothed off the cream, washed their legs with cold tea as a base colour, and patted them dry. Hazel giggled non-stop at the notion that drawing a penciled fake seam from ankle to underwear would fool anyone. "I'll do it," she told Jasmine, "but it's daft as a March hare in July."

Everyone knew that the supply of silk stockings was only for the rich these days. They'd hardly had a chance to get used to replacing them with nylon, when that option was taken away as well. At the cinema, the girls learned that 'Ripstop' nylon was found to be even more effective than silk. The newsreel showed long lines of factory workers, men and women, toiling at their sewing machines to turn huge patches of the stuff into parachutes, connecting ropes, and linings for Royal Air Force bomber jackets.

"Mum says some women get hold of parachute silk to make underwear."

To which Jasmine replied, "Now would that be rather risky or risqué, what do you reckon?"

They both focused on the decoration of their legs. Then Jaz asked, "You coming with me tonight?" Hazel looked interested. "Looking after that posh kid. You know, that place... other side of the Common. Looks like Buckingham Palace."

"Oh, yeah, Mansion House. Or something. I'd sooner be dancing!" She checked the back of her legs in the bedroom mirror. "Your turn, madam." Jasmine offered a limb.

"We'll have the run of the house. And we get to sleep over."

"I'll have to ask Mum, but should be fine. Doesn't Gran help out sometimes when they have dinner parties? Bit of cash in hand, I suppose."

Which is just what Jasmine's hoping for as well. "Actually, he's a sweetie, the little boy. Orlando."

"Jazzie, stop fidgeting!"

BLACKOUT

Even more than during The Great War, this one was throwing sand in the eyes of anyone trying to figure it out, make predictions, plan for the future. Confusion underpinned every aspect of life, and called into question the centuries old structure of society. The class system.

Students of history picking apart facts and artefacts knew better than any how periods of social transition foment discontent. On the surface, and especially because the British tended to live up to their stereotypes of politesse, stiff upper lip, and a Zen-like acceptance, feelings of resentment had been kept in check.

For the working class [not that one should over-generalise], centuries of deprivation and self-denial bred a sad resignation that this was their lot in life, no use resisting, nothing to be done.

Whereas the most privileged assumed the material advantages of their birth gave tacit leave to take whatever else they wanted. It's not that they were particularly bothered by the effects their actions had on the poor, they simply didn't regard them at all. They were -- to all intents and purposes -- invisible.

As for those caught in the social in-between, they were the most vulnerable. Aspirations upward tempted them unduly to sacrifice morality for personal gain; they studied and imitated the more covert illegalities of the wealthy. Crimes of money manipulation, investment fraud. While those on a downward spiral – by dint of debt, illness, or other disaster – were more attracted to less pre-meditated crimes. Bish, bash, bosh. Smash and grab. Opportunistic. The results were the same.

First in the East End, then through cobbled alleys up West, young lads could earn a farthing. They were known as The Bow Street Regulars, a parody on the police spies in those magazine serials. Or The Baker Street Boys. Mostly they ran behind the action, but lately they pedaled close to the kerb, on reconnoiter. The bicycles were left out for the ARP wardens, but as we know, war brought a different morality. Was it theft if lives were saved?

Some of the lads called themselves the Cycle Gang. They needed their wits about them through the fog, and it helped if they could spot dodgy deals sealed with a handshake. Spies and counter-spies. Some game! When the Gang was issued with exploding 'pineapples,' they had to devise ways and means for them to malfunction. Sadly, some hit their target, of course. Only human. Mistakes were inevitable.

Families heard the treble-voiced clarity of their queen declare she was glad the West End had suffered enemy attack; it made her feel less guilty about the decimation of entire East End streets. None of the announcements nor any short clips in the cinema newsreels delved into more suspect alliances: between members of the royal family, their friends and more distant relatives with the British Union of Fascists, the ubiquitous Brown shirts, the covert meetings on occupied ground with Nazi sympathisers, and the invitations to teas and garden parties in the balmy Bahamas where the deposed king had been re-assigned as the official Ambassador, and his right-wing wife curried favour with German plantation owners... old money mixing with its own kind.

After The Great War, no wonder the Queen's family were keen to distance themselves in the eyes of the British public from the Saxe-Coburg line of her great-great-grandmama Queen Victoria, and changed their name. Windsor has such a reassuring British sound.

BLACKOUT

"Where's Matt?" Myrtle asked Rose. "Haven't seen him all day."

"Wasn't he going up to London?" She explained that Izzy was lodging with her relatives in Stepney, and Matt wanted to spend more time with her before she went back to the Sorbonne. He'd also made Rose promise not to tell a soul, but he was fair bursting with the news he meant to propose. He showed his sister the ring he'd fashioned, etching intertwining lines into the gold plate.

She was genuinely impressed, even more that he'd made it himself than by the ring. They'd long gone beyond the childhood days she'd teased her little brother. "It's beautiful, Matt. She'll love it."

But he knew better than to reveal that some of Izzy's family were Jewish. It wasn't the best time to be Jewish, though, Matt asked himself, "What does everyone think we're fighting this war for?" He also failed to reveal that Izzy had joined the Communist Party. Matt knew it definitely wasn't the best time for that either.

BLACKOUT

They were playing hide-and-seek. Lando kept giving himself away with his giggle and chesty coughing. Hazel gave Jas a signal to look down a long corridor, wood-paneled walls displaying portraits of Lady Honora's ancestors. They'd turned on the lights in every room they entered. Never gave it a thought.

Jasmine put on a scary voice. "I'm coming to get you."

Orlando was clutching his rubber ball, but he let it go. He'd opened a hidden door in the paneling. It led to a staircase. The ball bounced down into a vast storage room. The girls chased their young charge to the bottom, all collapsing into a giggling heap. When they caught their breath and looked around, they didn't have to say anything. Here was treasure indeed.

And then the bomb fell upon them.

BLACKOUT

It certainly wasn't deliberate, and no one made any connection, but Felix and Onnie were hit both in town and country. On the very same evening they were dining at Simpsons, one of the Cycle Gang lobbed a grenade into the forecourt of the Savoy. It was no mere provocation, but carried out in order to foil German plans to plant and explode bombs on every floor of the Hotel. And it certainly wasn't deliberate that they'd parked their own shiny saloon several streets away, undamaged when they came to collect it. Was it?

On that very same evening, the Luftwaffe carried out Hitler's orders to fly a few in-an-out raids to shake the composure of rural residents. One wing of the Humble's Mansion House took a direct hit.

There were a series of underground tunnels through the West End. One led from Simpsons into the Savoy basement. When the waiter appeared to top up their champagne, he whispered news of the hotel forecourt explosion. Felix gave a curt nod and smiled at his wife. A few moments later they heard the air raid sirens. Onnie looked around anxiously. "Drink up, darling, and follow me."

The basement of the Savoy was fitted out with colour-coded comfy cubicles to assure that diners caught in an air raid, could rest in luxury. Sir Felix had been in on the planning phase, modifying the hotel's world class standards during The Great War.

Onnie couldn't tell where the music was coming from, but it had the desired effect. Keep calm and carry on. She hugged her husband. "Well, this is a nice surprise." She settled back into an armchair, waiting for the all clear. Before Felix joined her she saw him cross the room, meeting a uniformed member of the hotel staff. He passed over a thin parcel wrapped in brown paper; Felix placed it in his jacket pocket.

He stepped behind Onnie and put his hands over her eyes. "Hmm," she giggled, eagerly joining the guessing game, "let me see... are you Mr Douglas Fairbanks? Or Mr Hardy Amies? Or could you be my darling husband?!" Instead of an answer, Felix uncovered her eyes and dropped the thin parcel into her lap. She looked around.

"Well, go ahead. Open it."

Inside the wrapping were two pairs of real silk stockings. No kohl stick lines for Lady Honora! But, thrilled as she was, she did know they were considered contraband. "Wherever did you get these, Felix?" His response was an index finger over his lips, the gesture to Shh!

BLACKOUT

Ever since his election to lead his party of so-called Social Democrats, Hitler assumed taking full charge of the military came with the job. And, if it didn't, he assumed it anyway. It took him several years to complete the jig-saw of an all-out naval attack on Great Britain, but he'd only recently shared his audacious plans with a small panel of advisors. He called it operation Sea Lion. Many of the advisors, far more experienced in the ballet of warfare, called it naval gazing. No small irony. Some, all too well aware that the British were proving far more resistant than the 'puny Poles,' urged their Fuhrer to put the Sea Lion back in its cage for the time being. Feed it some fish.

"We just need a bit more testing. And more air support." By which time Hitler turned his gaze to the east. He was determined to cure the Soviets of their naughty ways, wanted to bomb them to Slavic smithereens. Where Napoleon had failed, the Aryans would triumph. The element of surprise, he told the advisors. Shock and awe. Though, his panel wondered, how much surprise could there be under skies that stretched on forever into the steppes and tundra and taiga? They'd see the army a mile off!

BLACKOUT

Matt helped Izzy lift the blood-red banner advertising the Stepney Young Communist League. Joining scores or more of their fellow marchers they knew where to find the shelter denied to them by government officials. All around, the streets of their childhood were on fire, their neighbours homeless. For too many months they'd been fobbed off by the Minister for This and the Minister for That. No one in government was prepared to alienate the uber-rich money pots who'd put them in power. Resources were not to be spent on the poor.

No, they couldn't have funds to dig down for deep shelters of safety. Absolutely not! And no, they wouldn't consider the Communists' sensible suggestion to open up the underground, not even for women and children. The homeless would just have to kip down with relatives. Or move to the countryside. Or sleep on the pavement; it wasn't all that cold. Pronouncements made from the cosy well-heated offices of well-heeled gentlemen. Written on vellum paper, stamped into officialdom. Sir Felix had many times taken tea with these men; he agreed the welfare of the wealthy must take priority. The old ways were the best ways, no matter how modern the times.

Izzy and Matt cheered with the rest at the passionate words of the speakers, bolstering their courage. They'd read with growing rage the calls for social justice printed repeatedly in the left-wing newspaper *The Daily Worker*. "If you live in the Savoy Hotel, you are called by telephone when the sirens sound and then tucked into bed by servants in a luxury bomb-proof shelter. But if you live in Paradise Court you may find yourself without a refuge of any kind. The people must act." And so they did.

BLACKOUT

Rose had packed some fish paste sandwiches into Arthur's cycle bag. His schedule that night took in the houses behind the Common, and the criss-cross of lanes leading back into town. The Mansion House was also on his list. He knew the shortcut through the copse that opened out to the wide gravel driveway, lined with oaks, tall firs, and clipped hedges. As he pedaled up to the house itself, he could hear Orlando's relentless crying. Impossible not to breathe in that pungent burning smell. The damage was devastating.

Arthur jumped from his bicycle, not caring how it fell. He raced to his daughter who was holding tight to the little boy trying to soothe him. So many rooms in the house blazed with light, not a curtain was drawn. The whole place was in criminal violation of the blackout, which might have been severe enough to take immediate action. But the most pressing matter was the gaping hole in the roof, that passing gift from the bomb of a German fighter pilot.

"Daddy, Jaz is buried... you have to find her."

Arthur forced some clear thought through the rising panic he felt. "Shh, darling. It's all right, Daddy's here." And after sharing water from his thermos with Hazel and the boy, he asked where Sir Felix and Lady Honora were.

He was proud of his daughter, coping like a grown-up. "I think they went to London. Jazzie knows. We've got to get her out."

Lando had calmed down and seemed content munching on a bit of fish paste sandwich with one hand while holding tight to Hazel with the other. They watched Arthur scramble down the rough slabs of plaster and bricks that tumbled together into the vast room beneath. Finally they heard Jasmine's feeble cry for help. "There! There she is!" shouted Hazel. "We're coming Jazzie, we're coming!"

It took some digging and much moving of debris, but at last the trapped girl was free. Dress torn, only one shoe, some blood and bruising all over. She and her rescuer lay back on the grass, panting for their breath. It was almost an afterthought that Arthur stood at last, peered down into the ruin and saw the contents for what they were.

Huge produce boxes stacked one atop another. An odour of apples mixing with charred crates. Wooden chests broken by the bomb, drawers open to reveal gems that glistened in the moonlight. Wardrobes that had lost their doors, protecting ball gowns and gentlemen's dress suits. A few whole sides of beef, slipped down from sturdy hooks to the stone floor, covered with ash. Such stockpiling had long been declared illegal. This wasn't just the stash of a week or two.

"We didn't mean to go down there, sir. We were chasing after Lando's ball." Jasmine was trying to balance, but her legs had been too badly crushed. She craved forgiveness even more than medical attention... though the torn skin would harden and scar, and she'd walk with a limp from then on. Far too embarrassed to meet up again to cut a rug with Lance. The lad was bereft, he really liked her, and only learned the truth years later. He'd given up by then. Another case of 'what might have been.' The minor tragedies of war that shave off bits of what some folk call the soul.

Arthur was still staring past her into the roofless basement. "Aladdin's Cave," he muttered under his breath. Aloud he said, "I wonder whether there's a working telephone in that far wing. Let's go investigate, shall we?" He knew he'd have to report this to someone. The sooner the better.

BLACKOUT

Now what, you may well wonder, what qualities the press baron of one of Britain's most popular newspapers possesses to qualify him to be appointed Minister for Supply. True, that position was yet to come, but It's no secret that Mr Aitken OBE helped change the course of the war. It would be his responsibility to procure the best deals for the military on everything from soup to nuts, as they said in his native Canada. It was at his lavish Surrey residence that he assembled like-minded news barons, fellow influencers to plot and plan, to use his private telephone network, circumventing unwelcome scrutiny, and to forge alliances with those who thrived on questionable acquisitions. No questions asked. Clandestine. Sir Felix, whom many considered rather young though most agreed on his loyalty, proved a popular guest.

Neither the newspapers nor the BBC wireless reported the incident that eventually came to be called the Stepney Invasion. It wasn't for another few decades that the real story could be told. Those in the know definitely knew. They knew the marchers not only had inside knowledge, but inside help as well... the unintended consequence of West End premises hiring cheaper East Enders or immigrants, restricting them like slaves, and wondering why their staff loyalty might desert them.

There was almost a party atmosphere in the Savoy basement shelter. Not raucous, heaven forfend, but what they called refined, worthy of their class. Suddenly they were aware of insistent shouting coming from the upstairs entry door. They couldn't make out every word, but the tone said it all. Threats and barriers from the hotel heavies, completely overwhelmed by the fired-up Stepney crowd. Izzy and Matt were near the front, their banner now furled as a battering ram. They were approached by a hefty bull of a man, married to one of Izzy's cousins. He pretended to rail at them, pretended to push them away back against the others. But look carefully. He was actually opening the door wider and shoving them through. Pretending to be cowed by their sheer persistence.

The marchers carried on downstairs met by the sound of screams. Not so polite, now. Shrill with panic, and not just the women. But Sir Felix never wavered. He had his own insiders. Once again he led Onnie through the mob. As they hurried past to the exit, Matt and Lady Honora recognised each other. She was such a prominent figure in town, and his comings and goings were frequently the subject of gossip.

Not much got past Izzy. "Who was that?"

"From the town. He's a top cheese, so is she."

"They won't get far; the streets are crawling with us Stepney folk!"

But through the alleyways of threat and terror, Felix led Onnie to their trusty roadster. As she caught her breath, Felix double-checked the catch on the boot. She couldn't see, but there was cargo. Oh, yes there was!

They confronted a certain amount of chaos on the road home which had been strafed in the raid. But Felix improvised as though he had a map in his head. With some side turnings and even a double-back, they arrived at their Mansion House driveway...

where they were stopped by the county police and placed under arrest. The large box of contraband supplies and munitions in the boot was taken into evidence.

Felix protested that Lady Honora had nothing to do with this, urging them to 'let her go'. He was right; she knew nothing, could barely look at her husband, his arms behind his back, secured by handcuffs. He assumed she was smiling at him for support. He was wrong; it was no smile. Her only thought was to get to Lando.

"Let me go. I'm his mother, he needs me!"

BLACKOUT

With all the stress, she miscarried and the nursery remained unused. They moved into her mother's Mayfair townhouse, plenty of room. The family closed ranks, put on a public face. No one apart from Felix and Onnie needed any details; she, however, knew her choice of separate bedrooms from then on was self-defense. There was a trial. Eventually. Sir Felix Humble versus The Crown. The docket might as well have been headed Privilege and Pay-off versus Don't Waste Our Time. Despite all the evidence, the testimony, the witnesses, somehow the record shows the blame fell on the Communists and East End rabble.

Nothing, as we know, was reported in the right-of-centre papers. Instead, they dripped stories of an imminent Luftwaffe attack across Great Britain. The aim was to keep selling papers, of course, but people trusted Mr Aitken and his press pals, and everyone looked anxiously over their shoulders, some even spending entire days in their bunkers. Flames that fueled their fighting spirit sputtered, threatened to go out. The Stepney crowd put on a brave face, but they were all disheartened. In fact, there were some half-hearted attacks on the offices of the *Daily Worker*. Rumour had it the paper was in danger of being shut down. Matt and Izzy had close contacts in the French resistance. They decided to brave the journey to Paris where they married without much ceremony but hearts full of love. They posed for photographs and sent a couple to Myrtle. Time can accommodate the bigger picture and the snapshots.

THE ALL CLEAR

The children were left the house to sell or divide as they wished. Rose and Arthur found Matt's photos in her mother's cedar cigar box when they cleared the house after her death in the mid-1970s. They parroted that clichéd cricket analogy: "She had a good innings." Jasmine also lent a hand; she'd moved in with her big sister, rarely venturing out. She felt defiled by her limp and the scarring.

Hazel's bedroom was empty since she'd joined a hippy commune in London. She moved around a lot, but always let them know where to get in touch. Arthur went up to visit a couple of times; gave her some photos of John and the younger boys, Basil whose name she'd chosen and Ronnie. Neither father nor daughter had been able to banish the images of that night the Germans attacked. Today there were new alliances.

Basil, now a skinny family man in his thirties turned up to help. Happy memories when Rose had brought him along to visit his "Ganny," as he'd called her. Always a slice of cake on offer. As Rose often said, "This kid can eat for England. I don't know where he puts it all!" Basil's baby brother Ronald had recently qualified as a veterinary surgeon and opened a practice with his wife's father up in the Lake District. He'd made time for the funeral, but they all understood he had to get back. All so proud. Hard to see him now -- beard neatly trimmed, just a hint of grey -- without remembering Ronnie, the wee boy.

The odour of the war lingered, though pure truth would take longer to reveal itself. John Lennon was imagining people living in peace, but they were still dying and fighting, however many miles away. Didn't speak the lingo, but the blood's the same colour. Along the High Street life carried on much as always. Some tears and some shared joys. As they'd sung in days past: 'The rich get richer and the poor get children.'

Rose showed Basil more photographs of Matt and Izzy's twins, Rowen and Daisy. More Flower Girls. There was still a faint whiff of cedar from the cigar box.

***

CHAPTER EIGHT – INSPECT & VERIFY

The Collective Invention 1934 Rene Magritte

Rene Magritte's intriguing painting, Collective Invention, inspired this short story. Considered by some the supremo of surrealism, Magritte presents this bizarre creature to evoke not only the mythos of its subject but as a challenge to the very notion of the male gaze.

When he painted it in 1934, many women who'd taken so called men's work during WW1, were having to reconcile being redefined back to domesticity. As a proto-feminist Magritte wanted men to look again, his own vision compromised by the drowning by suicide of his mother when he was just thirteen.

Inspect & Verify

The Inspector glanced at the wall clock in his private office. Belt and braces and by the book, he synchronised the time against his own wrist watch. The papers on his desk needed no further initialling nor straightening, and he slipped them into the top drawer. He peeked through the window blind. All clear, no umbrella required. In short, released from the day, he could head for home. All that was left was to put on his jacket. And then the telephone rang.

A light bird-like sound. Brring-brring. He almost left it unanswered. He could. No one would dare to stop him. He could step into the corridor, leaving the door ajar for the cleaner, and parade past the labs and offices that comprised his domain. The odd wave, a nod of the head. He could. The phone chirped again. But he just couldn't. It might be some emergency.

The Inspector left his jacket on the door hook, brushed a hand across his thinning brown hair – a habitual gesture - and returned to his desk. He reached across for the receiver and pressed the flashing button. Like some arbitrary *son-et-Lumière* show, the light was out of synch with the ringing. He paid mind to stuff like that; he wasn't called The Inspector for nothing. If he had hopes of dismissing the caller, curt but polite, the incessant verbiage at the other end stopped the words dead in his mouth. He flipped the telephone cord over the desk and sat down for the news.

*

The sea was mauve as a Rose of Sharon by the time the Inspector trudged over the last of the duned ridges. He was not a happy bunny. This was his final call out for the day. Unscheduled. A last-minute add-on.

He paused to roll up his trouser legs, and knock the sand from his shoes against his briefcase. Using his hand as a sunshade, he scanned the shoreline for the rendezvous point. A smudged pale band on the horizon might burst into a multi-coloured sunset or sink without ceremony behind the sea. It was too far away to tell. He could make out a small dinghy pulled onto the beach. Nearby, a white-coated figure had its back turned, but was, he assumed, the Professor. He was bent over something stretched out before him, the soft waves lapping around them. From this distance they looked like toys on a table.

He was a man of lists and order; by rights he should already be on his way home. But the information he'd received from Joyce, the Academy receptionist, was delivered with such urgency, such intrigue, that immediately he knew he had to attend. Personally. It was no place for eager assistants and associates aiming to share credit on his yet-to-be-written presentation paper to the Academy. After all, he'd been working on the case for... he calculated on his fingers... almost seven years.

Not ego, he justified to his devil voice. A matter of propriety. But both he and his conscience knew exactly what was at stake. Does the name Nobel mean nothing anymore?

He pulled the mobile phone from his jacket, grateful for a clear signal at last and a full-bar charge. He rang his wife with instructions to delay supper.

"But Harold," she protested. "Fish and chips, your favourite." The phone image didn't do justice to her disappointment.

"Now Dora love, you know how important this is..." He tried as hard as he could to resist the plea in her adorable blue eyes. Adorable Dora.

"Crispy cod in soda water batter," she interrupted, hoping against hope. He blew her a digital kiss.

Ce n'étaient pas ses yeux. Those were not her eyes... only an image of them. His own peepers were pale, not weak and watery, but steady as a rock pool. Prussian blue was her colour. Deep, dark, with naughty promises of midnight. He'd inspected and verified it with the assistance of his lab team. It was quite definitely a multi-use pigment. "Double dip chips," she said, the temptress.

She was right. It was his favourite meal. And her chips were to die for. None better, not even on the High Street. "I'll try to be quick."

A sudden wheeling of wings and a skimming of waves caught his attention. Too far away to threaten, but you never knew. He could definitely feel the blast of a breeze and was glad he'd listened that morning to Dora to slip his vee-necked sleeveless jumper over his shirt. She was always right. He smoothed down his hair and moved closer to the sea.

When he was within shouting distance, the man stood to face him, his voluminous lab-coat still blocking most of the figure behind. There, unmistakably, was a human foot. Two human feet. The Professor beamed his greeting, waved his arms from side to side. Assuming the worst, the Inspector's shoulders sagged. "Hullo there!" he bellowed across the sand.

*

He could recall every detail of their first meeting. He and Dora were combining their Halloween honeymoon cruise along the Rhine with a stopover at the thirteenth century castle of Lord Konrad the Second, Reiz von Breuberg. The former ruin, recently renovated, was fast gaining a reputation as a wedding venue, and hosted an annual Horror Night celebration. Fun for the whole family.

As his former typist and transcriber, Dora was well aware that her newly wedded husband's interest was more specific. Inspect and verify. A cultural alliance: inspection fulfilled the demands of Science, but verification was an Art.

True, together they'd confirmed the application of Prussian Blue as a brand-new pigment, synthetically available not just for painters, but now vital for industrial chemists and breakthrough medical applications in the treatment of radiation poisoning. Which is how Johann Konrad Dippell came to their attention. Well, he came to the Inspector's attention. Dora was too busy transcribing his notes to leave time for speculation. No surprise that his handwriting followed every curve and peak of legibility, but he did tend to get carried away into the jungle of syntax.

Dippell had indeed been born in the castle, but what made him so fascinating was his obsession with the ancient alchemists, ever seeking the fabled elixir of life. He was convinced his experiments with distillations of animal oil, squeezed from the sebaceous glands of mammals, birds, and lizards in precise combinations, would result in a transfer of the dead into the living. Could he mix a mouse with a meadow lark, a toad with a tortoise? He wanted to engineer the human soul. No more, no less.

The Inspector took his work very seriously. When the Academy requested his expertise, he set to with a mind open to possibilities, putting scepticism aside. The pathway of Science was littered with overthrown theories, species once believed to be the stuff of dreams, and those still under scrutiny.

Harold and Dora both entered into the spirit of Horror Night. They'd come prepared with appropriate costumes packed with their luggage. She helped him into a ragged suit, held together with a strand of rope around his waist, holes carefully ripped into the arms and legs. He adjusted a moulded rubber mask painted with cheeks of putrid green and a livid scar splitting one eye.

"Smile," said Dora, and she rubbed liquorice paste across his front teeth. "Perfect," she said, holding the mirror for his approval. "Truly monstrous." Her own get up was more basic: a wrap-around black cloak topped with a pointed witch's hat. She carried a small whisk broom. Her little joke. She'd have to be shrunk down like fairy-tale Alice to ride around on that! Arm in arm they disembarked at the river pier, strolling across the castle lawn to join the party crowd.

Harold scanned around for a sight of the Professor, his concentration broken by a nudge from his wife. "Look at them." She was chuckling at a family of ghosties, arms linked and singing, all in disguise with bed-sheets and cut-out eye holes, one clamped by a pair of glasses. "A ghost in specs!"

Some children, laughing and pushing, gathered round a barrel to bob for apples. A furry-suited black cat, walking on two legs, removed its head to sip mulled wine. Dora smiled at her, and Harold could smell the spice. From a billowing tent, tethered to the ground, came the oompah beat of unseen accordions. It didn't take long for them to succumb to the tang of barbequed meat, a sweet-smoked treat. Fun for all the family.

While Dora filled two plates from the buffet, Harold sought out the Professor. He wasn't hard to spot. Dressed in his lab coat but otherwise un-costumed, he stood on the polished stone staircase, playing both the welcoming host and a barrier to unwanted exploration inside. "Please," he insisted, "Call me Viktor." Harold knew that Dippell had adopted the name of his long-dead ancestor, Doktor Frankenstein.

Harold introduced himself. If the rumours were true, this was an opportunity not to be missed. They skipped past the small talk. Two professionals getting down to business. It took only a few minutes for the Professor to confirm his latest plans. "Yes, I'm working on a brand-new composite creature. I take inspiration from myth." And leaning closer to Harold, he whispered just one word. Then he put his forefinger to his lips. "Shh," he said.

"Have you... have you had any success?" Harold could barely keep the flame of anticipation from his voice.

"A matter of trial and error, sir. Trial and error." He waved an arm to include the many couples and families, the tent, and all the coloured lanterns. "I relish your presence at our little celebration." His eyes widened with the excitement. "I will prove all science a tainted beast."

Harold was wise enough to know the Professor had not actually said anything, nothing he could close in his hand and take away with him. But the door was ajar, he could see that much. "Well," he said, "I look forward to learning of your... developments."

That was the moment Dora found them. He took the plate of food she offered, and when he looked back at the Professor, he'd been joined by another man dressed unconvincingly as a pumpkin. They were deep in conversation. Harold and Dora melted into the crowd.

*

Over the years the Professor had sent the occasional letter to Harold, none relating any actual progress. Lately these had dwindled to just an annual postcard with the word 'Hopeful' and signed 'Viktor.' Dora had duly filed them away, and Harold all but forgot them entirely.

Now here he was. His footprints cupping into the yielding sand. Edging closer to the Professor, to the streaks of purple sky. And further from his supper.

The beached dinghy rocked with the tide. Balanced inside was a shallow tank filled with clear water. "Ta-dah!" The Professor gestured a presentation to the body stretched out on the damp sand. Its mouth bubbled with the effort of... could it be speech? Was it trying to say something?

The Inspector swallowed back the watery vomit that filled his mouth. He didn't dare ask what bloody demonic hell confronted him there and then, but whatever it was, he knew it wasn't Science. He wiped his lips with the handkerchief in his pocket and found his voice. "Viktor," he said with a vicious calm. "What have you done?"

"Isn't she wonderful?" The Professor circled the creature, almost dancing with delight. "I've been working on her for nearly a year, kept all the notes. Of course, there's lots more to do, she's far from perfect. But what do you think? Will you verify? Is she ready for The Academy?"

The Inspector forced himself to take another look. The pair of naked legs that met in a female triangle, its dark curly hair blended into the fish scales of its upper body. The lips longing for a different element. He set down his briefcase and removed his jacket. Taking hold of both feet he gestured Viktor round to the head. Instead of raging and shouting in despair, he spoke calmly. "Let's get her into the water, poor thing, before she suffocates."

Together they lifted her up and waded into the water, releasing her with care, a rare species. They watched her legs kick out, propelling her across the waves. Her head bobbed up, and she looked back at them, before diving down out of sight.

The Professor reached out toward her, an impotent gesture. “But… but… We agreed. You said that’s what you wanted. We agreed.”

“No, Professor,” said Harold. “That is not at all what I meant by a mermaid.”

The Inspector was in no mood to continue the pretense of civility with the demented Professor. The wind raced across the water toward them. He smoothed down the hair across his forehead and hastily fastened his jacket.

*

Briefcase in hand, he negotiated the dunes back to the car park. What a bizarre evening! Dora would never believe it.

***

KWICKIE KAPTION 5

American born James Abbott McNeill Whistler [1834 – 1903] spent most of his career in the United Kingdom, where he sought a greater freedom to paint without having to please others. Intrigued by the relationship between art and music, he chose titles more commonly applied to composition, such as Arrangement or Nocturne. His most famous portrait is officially called *Arrangement in Grey and Black No. 1*, but far better known as Whistler's Mother.

Quite coincidentally, his trademark autograph includes a butterfly with a sting in its tail.

If that kid doesn't stop whistling,
I swear I'm going to give him such a slap!

CHAPTER NINE – A TINY TURN

Escaping Dichroism: The Two Suns 2019 Beth Porter

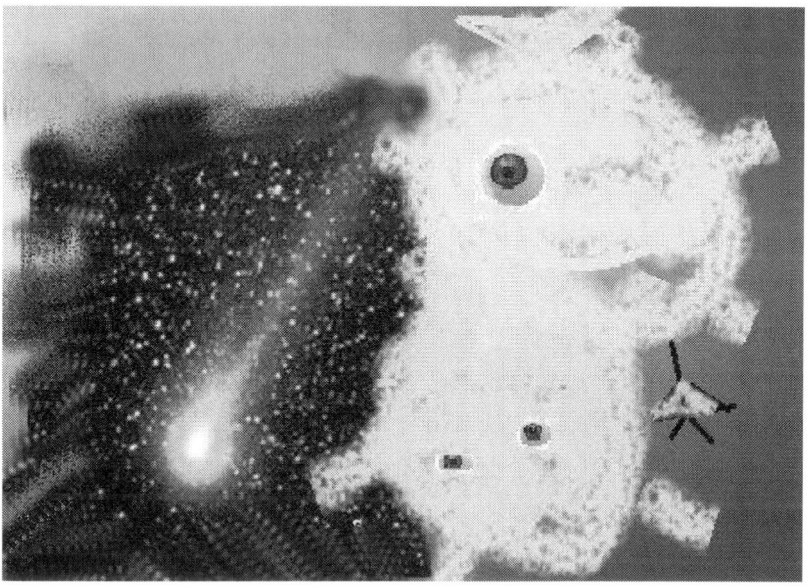

One of the joys of compiling these stories inspired by well-known images has been to put them into context. I've been able to better understand the lives of the artists, whether men or women, and undertake detailed research to assure accuracy.

Restricted quite rightly by more recent copyrighted portraits, I'm not able to make royalty payments. My only option, therefore, has been to create my own image for this final piece of flash fiction, set in a fabricated future. I've tried to tame my rage into something more hopeful. The rage is at myself, as well as all of us, though for decades I've been writing about the dangers of our profligate ways. It's driven by my passion for the very survival of Earth in the face of our collective and shameful neglect, and is my version of marching under the banner of Extinction Rebellion.

It's meant to complement the book's first offering, *The Sitting*. Angelika Kauffmann's extraordinary portrait cunningly captures the relationship between artist and subject, and is both of its era and universal. I wanted my own image to reduce the narrative to a digital simplicity. The Tiny Turn of the title is meant to evoke the potential chromatic power inside a kaleidoscope from so small a movement.

The setting just barely acknowledges the confusion of people trying to understand the effects of climate change and continued loss of bio-diversity. It presents a hazy vision, recreated through the eyes of a child.

Representational art surviving hundreds of thousands of years, has been shown to be far more sophisticated than the callow analyses documented in more recent, more arrogant centuries. But contrasted with examples of very young children's artwork across cultures, age is the key differential. Most babies just aren't interested in drawing and painting, usually producing squiggles or colour blobs before being diverted elsewhere.

Research by developmental psychologists proves that it's only when children reach three or four that they have the inclination and skill to draw versions of the people they see around them. These are commonly identified by rudimentary signals of gender, such as hair-bows for females.

My 'portrait' uses various digital paint effects to approximate a child's crayon rendition of a 'lady sun,' positioning it alongside the distorted context of the night sky. These are both fiendishly confusing concepts for people trying to find a path to a brighter future from the chaos created by their previous disastrous choices.

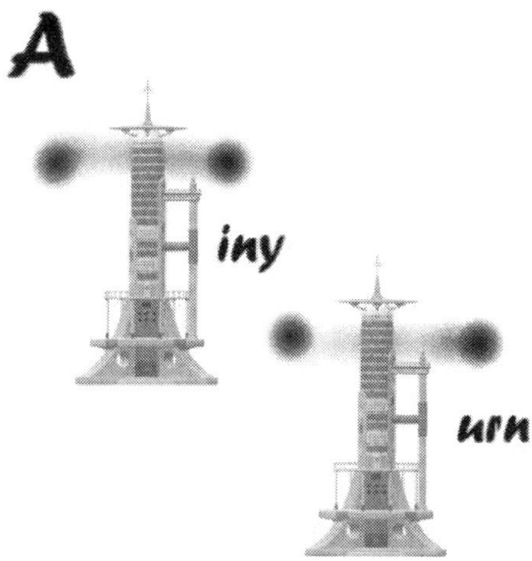

Everyone's a Roamer these days, doesn't matter where they came from. Sometimes the clouds tear apart like badly sewn seams, and the sky shines uninterrupted. Nobody quite remembers when their blurred memories of daylight and their dreams took on the defining label: The Land of the Two Suns.

If they thought about it at all, they guessed it must have been a consequence of the days of destruction. Glacier melts, ocean churnings, storm surges, inundated islands… all the warnings were dismissed as scare-mongering and just ignored. The Time Before The Beyond. To be fair, they all had enough to think about just surviving.

Convinced they could buy their way out, do a deal, the biggest, and barricade themselves into a golden refuge, they soon found they couldn't escape such persistent havoc. It blew the roofs off their sky-palaces and the wigs off their heads.

An important announcement! Not a single one of the soothsayers and gazers into globes of phony crystal from Nostradamus to that 1960s Manhattan doomster parading a sign proclaiming The End is Nigh – not one has ever been able to predict the future.

Strange but true: if you look back much, much further, some of our ancestors could do exactly that. They themselves may have learned lessons from the creatures around them, or they may have evolved the facility by applying the advantages of evolution. Something compelled them to make mental survival maps and share them with their anthropoid pals... maps that predicted not only the exact place, but also the exact time that yummy fruit and vital fresh water would appear. When you consider that some trees, for example, only provide their sweet goodness every two or three years, I hope you'll agree our canny ancestors must be congratulated.

Such a shame our current arrogance has replaced those valuable basics. And there's the matter of pronoun referral, not that it matters too much, but it may not be what you expect in a narrative. You read about 'they' and 'them,' mostly as a collective of thought and action, the journey more telling than the actors. You shouldn't get lost; they've left such helpful footprints.

Not everyone got carried away by relentless waters. But survivors looking to the sky, wherever they happened to be at the time, however hard they rubbed at their eyes, there they were. Two Suns. A trick of the light, perhaps, explained by a scrupulous study of the science of prisms? Hardly anyone left to call it dichroism.

Before the current attempts at map-making, the general consensus was to spend their energy navigating to some drinkable water. Before it was too late. Everyone knew someone who had perished during the decades of treacherous tides, wildfire, drought and ignorance. Sadly, it was a pretty random affair, putting horse before cart as we used to say. They believed that once their collective thirsts were slaked, then they could gather together to design longer-term plans. Cope. Escape.

*

The butterflies were back. A miracle of sorts. Not many remembered the last time the air had turned orange and lemony-pale with the beating of their tiny wings. The young ones had to be told what they were. "Birds?"

The insects clumped together to rest in the branches of trees. Remarkable fruit. In fact, trees and fruit had only just begun making a comeback of their own. "No. Not birds," said their mums and dads. "You know, love, whatcha-callems - fluttery, no buttery - oh, you know!" The grans and grand-dads smiled in their knowledge and said, "Butterflies."

Looking back, telling the tales again and again, they'd made so many mistakes, taken so many bad turnings, it was a wonder they were still around. No one spoke it aloud, but whenever they confronted a pile of bleached bones, they slowed down and stared in silence. A legacy of sorts. Telling the tales as they sat around the night-time fire.

It had taken quite a jolt to get them to move about, to explore, to set aside their fear of the hills. Silly really, but why go if you don't have to. Until you do have to. When the land became as stingy as a slave driver, the choice excluded all but the going. "But where..." they couldn't bear to finish the thought.

"This way," said the old folks, now just a few still with them. "We've been before. This way."

But the landscape had changed, their wells were running dry. Finally, after months of hit and miss, they remembered where the water was. “Make a map,” insisted the others. Finally a helpful suggestion! No one wanted to die in a drought. Nowadays, as soon as the streams began to cake into mud shapes, they packed their tents and made a beeline for the Well Lands.

*

The natural world, like a master magician, always has a trick or two up its voluminous sleeve. You’ve seen it yourself, when [just to take a rather mundane example] drops, sheets, even torrents of rain fall onto one side of the street, while the other side stays dry as an abandoned bone.

After the floods, when the coastlines surrendered to the sea and the planet's polarity flipped, the counting began. The survivors, accustomed from birth to calculate quantity, still hadn't understood to value quality. But with the tally came the useful realisation that the very state of survival could be, should be, and would be the genesis of a brand new world. They still had to learn how to include all the surviving plants and animals together... crossing the boundaries of diversity and stepping over any remaining boundaries of geography or residual prejudice.

It was tough to shift from taxonomy to a tamer life. Naysayers paddled in the cold puddles of the past. But a kind of kindness was happening all over, smoothing out the days of warring tribes. They met on the mounds of their problems, all guidelines gone. They found ways to last, at last, to awake to each dawn of the two suns. They foraged, of course, but sought as well some signs they weren't alone. So, on they wandered.

Their journeys uncovered strange shapes, rusted, left from some distant era. All stirred memories, and a few were actually useful. When the coast pulled its waters back into the ocean, the remains of a ship's hull tempted exploration. By a process beyond their control it had evolved into a marine refuge, home to sea creatures that provided a tasty treat. Survival. And speaking of the phenomena of the shore, they didn't ignore a certain tree that toppled of its own accord. It landed in the water and, wonder of wonders, it floated. They rubbed their brains together and turned float into boat. Survival. And still they wandered. Survival and escape from devastation, from the Before Time. Could they carve out a future?

*

Turns out the future was further inland, not too far from the coast, on slightly higher ground. Took many months to get to the helpful steps carved into the rock, leftover from the Before Time. The rocks themselves used to push up into the clouds, but now they could be climbed in just an hour. Mountains no longer, some collapsed entirely, boulders breaking upon the riverbank. Yes, this was a place of water, and the hills were lined with trees and fruit and all the animals blended into a natural happiness. Perhaps the people were left overs. There weren't many, fifty or so. Enough to acquire names, well, more descriptors than names. Identities, though some did double-duty: Digger, Tracker, Poet, Cook, Engineer, Astronomer, Collector, Planner, Physician, Lover, Singer, Designer, Dancer. No hierarchies.

Every single one a teller of tales. Memories shared and stories dreamed in the mind. Perhaps they'd trekked from another place, escaping the floods, the droughts, the clashes with tyrants. Bankers and wankers, the path to these hills was lined with their heads displayed on spikes. Some knew who the enemy had been.

If you measure time by a hundred earth years, then what is left of the humans recognised three separate generations. They called themselves Denizens, and embraced any who cared to bide: human, animal, plant, and even the progeny of inter-species exchange. Experiments in unlikely helix matches. Incomers welcome. The Roamers became Settlers, called the old-timers Dennies, and were accepted with open arms. New blood nourished the gene pool, and they swam willingly. They were discovering new ways to live, to survive, to thrive.

Determined to explore a system devoid of predictable politics, they owed nothing to the past. One of their most rejected concepts was Leadership, which had proved a total con, enriching the few and stirring hatred among the many. Those who remembered the old ways, or even the stories about them, knew that nothing had worked. The whole approach was fashioned upon lies, setting folk against each other, endangering the very existence of all other life forms.

The bedrock of the Dennies' new philosophy was respect, especially for all living beings. They welcomed elders, mothers, dads, boys and girls, and cauliflowers. Wait... what? Cauliflowers?! Yeah, well, no, they knew they couldn't create a genetic combo of a nubile woman with the florets of a brassica.

But let's face it, there are certain problems that need extra guidance, and it might be wise to examine them from a different angle. In other words, it might be handy to think like a cauli. Or a whale. Or a butterfly. Nothing was out of bounds.

Neither you nor I can predict the future, but the Dennies were learning they had to concoct their lives from the secrets around them. Hidden in plain sight. After all, escape from devastation uncovers so many untrod roads.

What course would you follow? What do you think they should do? For, to tell you the truth, it really is your choice.

***

About Beth

Once upon a time I spent 6-months in a cage with two baby orangutans at the LA Zoo. This is true, but has nothing to do with my professional career. Read on!

Before graduating from university, New Yorker Beth began acting professionally at age 12, coming to prominence as part of the award-winning LaMaMa Troupe, led by Tom O'Horgan and Ellen Stewart. They invited Beth and her Scottish husband Peter Reid to co-found the Troupe's UK branch, touring throughout Europe. Her successful solo career in films & television includes featured roles in Woody Allen's *Love & Death; Tales of the Unexpected; Hitch-hiker's Guide To The Galaxy*; and ITV hit series *Rock Follies*.

Acting segued into media journalism as London Editor of *Film Journal International*; writing fiction plays; being appointed BBC-TV development executive; & working as exec producer of corporate websites for an international webhouse.

In 2002 Intellect Publishing brought out her book *The Net Effect*, a socio-cultural account of the internet, with a foreword by David Lord Puttnam.
Resident Aliens: stories of NYC in the 1960s was her first solo collection of short fiction, published in 2013, followed the next year by Drama Queen, a collection of original scripts and screenplays.

In April 2016 Beth published her autobiography *Walking On My Hands: how I learned to take responsibility for my life with the help of Woody Allen, Barbra Streisand, Greta Garbo, Harvey Milk, Idi Amin, Guy the Gorilla, & Frank Sinatra among others*. Its foreword is by Shane Connaughton, award-winning novelist and screenwriter of *My Left Foot.*

Later that year she published *Settling Beyond The Pale*, her 2nd collection of short fiction. In October 2017 she published, *Feeding the Twins*, a magical realism take on the horror genre.

ScreenSaver! was Beth's first published novel, a rom-com with a fantasy twist. Her second novel *Becca's Providing* explores themes of identity, love, and how our human family solves common problems.

Painted Ladies is Beth's 3rd collection of original short fiction, each story inspired by classic paintings of women through the ages. All her books are available on Amazon.

Printed in Poland
by Amazon Fulfillment
Poland Sp. z o.o., Wrocław

53708857R00108